8.95

Also by Wm. Stage

Ghost Signs: Brick Wall Signs In America
ST Publications, Cincinnati 1989

Mound City Chronicles
Hartmann Publishing Company, St. Louis 1991

Wm. Stage, B. Ph

LITCHFIELD

Illustrations by Robert Asher

Floppinfish Publishing Company, Ltd.
St. Louis

Floppinfish Publishing Company, Ltd.
P.O. Box 4932
St. Louis, Missouri 63108

For Dan Meins, my brother at arms

LITCHFIELD

Cover Design: Daniel Pearlmutter
Interior Design & Layout: David Henline
Copy Editing: Michael Kunz
Area Map: Geographic Solutions, Inc.
Portions of this work first appeared in
The Riverfront Times,
Hartmann Publishing Company, Inc.

Library of Congress Catalog Card Number:
97-095038

ISBN: 0-962-91241-7

Printed in the United States of America
June, 1998

Introduction

I have been interested in this case from the moment I heard the news on the radio one morning in Spring, 1993: Nude, headless body found burning in a Litchfield, Illinois campground. Even in a time when so little qualifies as shocking, this thing seemed so brutal, indeed monstrous, the act of discarding a human being in such callous fashion, that it was actually disturbing to think that someone would have the desire and the will to carry it out. Whoever did it, I mused, would have to be a truly twisted individual.

I met Curtis Thomas in 1985 while he operated the original Final Edition newsstand. We would never be friends, though we have several mutual friends and acquaintances. Still, I understand why people would like him. Curtis was engaging, literate and witty, an overall entertaining fellow to be around. He was also sneaky, insulting and narcissistic. Tell you a story about the man: Each week I produce a newspaper column, one of those candid camera photo-opinion features. Actually, I accost people on the street, asking them impertinent, if not foolish questions, and I remember cornering Curtis one day in 1989 and posing the question: "Are you working in your chosen field?" Without hesitation, he replied, "No, I'm supposed to be a major deity, but I'm waiting for an opening." I believe he was only half-joking.

Curtis has been called a con man, a bullshit artist, a shit-disturber and worse. But of all the labels, of all the descriptive sobriquets ever put on him, the truest perhaps was one I heard from a former roommate and co-worker of Curtis and that is megalomaniac.

An interesting choice of nouns, that, and one that Curtis with his mental-health background would appreciate. The only other person I've heard that term applied to was President Richard Nixon during his long and painful fall from grace. My Funk & Wagnall New Practical Standard Dictionary of the English Language, 1951 Edition, defines megalomaniac as "a mental disorder in which the subject thinks himself great or exalted." Sometimes megalomaniacs actually achieve leadership positions, driving themselves with fierce ambition, changing human history for better or for worse. Think of Napoleon Bonaparte, Katherine The Great, Idi Amin. But mostly, they simply walk around feeling pretty damned important, deluding themselves that the rest of the world feels the same way.

Curtis Lee Thomas, whose first aspiration was to be a president of the United States, may now have difficulty imagining himself exalted while wearing the orange jumpsuit of a state prisoner, having to eat, sleep and recreate at the commands of his keepers.

The man came very close to getting away with murder. The first trial, in Hillsboro, Illinois, for concealing a homicide, was the acid test of his guilt or innocence in the greater offense, the ultimate robbery, the taking of a life. By the conclusion of that first trial, the significant action surrounding this tragic play had already occurred: The characters had spoken their lines, the denouement had unfolded, the curtain had fallen.

Though prosecutors were determined to keep trying him for murder until they got it right, any future verdict would be almost academic. Curtis' conviction of the lesser crime would not exonerate him, in the public eye, from culpability in the murder of Lynne Matchem-

Thomas, because the two crimes, concealment of a homicide and the actual murder of that same victim, are as intertwined as a nest of hibernating rattlers. His character would be tainted with the blood of his wife and he would have to live with that.

Wm. Stage
February, 1998

Author's Note

What follows is a work of nonfiction. The events chronicled are true and the characters are real. No names have been changed. While much of the book is based on material taken from court files, trial transcripts and newspaper accounts, it is also based on casual interviews with people who were in some way involved with the case or simply knew the persons involved. Because trial testimony and personal interviews can produce conflicting versions of the same event, the author has tried to provide a version of the facts which is, in his opinion, the most plausible.

For the sake of dramatic effect the author has taken small liberties with the dialogue and thoughts of certain characters. Otherwise, the preponderance of scenes herein chronicled have been faithfully re-created from actual events.

"Lynne would come in, the whole house would light up. She was always laughing. If she was depressed you didn't know it.

"Down near the end, she came over with Curtis and they'd be arguing. She was scared and it changed her. I've never seen anyone change like that. She was afraid like she saw her death. She said something's going to happen."

— Shirley Matchem

" ... despite whatever you may have heard about the presumption of innocence, everyone accused of a crime is immediately diminished, transmogrified into something less than human, merely by being charged."

— Leslie Abramson

"Who are those who will eventually be damned? Oh the others, the others, the others!"

— The Roycroft Dictionary
and Book Of Epigrams

PART I

ONE

When Todd Burdell first noticed the arm sticking out of the burning brush, he thought it was a mannequin. It was a Saturday night in Litchfield, Illinois, just before 10:30, when Burdell and his girl-friend, Tami Jett, fishing on Lake Lou Yaeger, spotted a fire in a picnic area just off the main road that goes through the park. It was a sizeable fire and unattended. Burdell, worried about a forest fire, went to get camp-ground superintendent Paul Stevenson.

Stevenson lived in a small wood-frame house up the road, near the campground, the better to keep watch on things. He had just returned from locking up the restrooms in the park and was nearly settled in when he heard banging at the door. "Hey Stevie!" called Burdell to his friend. "We got a fire down at Picnic Area 5, a good one!" Stevenson was skeptical. He'd dri-ven past Picnic Area 5 no more than 15 minutes ago and there was no fire. "Well, hold your horses," Stevenson called back.

Stevie followed Burdell back to the blaze, now even larger. The two men began stamping out the edges of the fire. Then Burdell noticed something poking out of the burning brush and logs. What the hell! It looked like an arm – "Jesus, it's a mannequin," muttered Burdell – but the flames were too great to get close enough to see better. Burdell and Jett and Stevenson stood there for awhile watching the blaze, making sure it didn't spread. When the fire went down a bit, Stevie stepped into it. He grasped the arm-thing by the wrist, but it was too hot, and he let go. He went to get his gloves in the pickup. Again, Stevie and Burdell stepped into the fire, now nearly consumed. They both pulled on the arm and it gave a little, exposing a biceps and armpit. Like a slap, the rank smell of burning flesh assaulted them.

"My heart about jumped out of my chest," Burdell later told police.

They kicked at the logs. Beneath the brush and timber, they discovered the nude body of a woman. Her head was hacked off at the shoulders and much of her legs and torso were charred. It was a very nasty piece of business.

They pulled her body from the fire and dragged it about 15 feet to the gravel drive that lead into the picnic area. "I guess it ain't no mannequin," said Stevie, eyes fixed on the dark, contorted shape.

Stevie jumped in his pickup and drove down to the Marina where his boss, Jim Kirby, lived. "Jim, you won't believe this ..." Stevie began. Kirby radioed the police, and that was the start of a long night.

It was May 8, 1993, prom night in Litchfield. The cops were expecting the usual shenanigans — cars getting egged, a few houses getting TP'ed — but this, this was a scene from *Fright Night* or some other slasher movie. Randy Quinn with the Litchfield Police Department was one of the first at the scene. He, too, thought he was seeing a department-store mannequin. "It was hard to believe at first," he recalled. "She just didn't look real."

Then came the Illinois State Police (ISP) evidence techs, the homicide investigator on call, the police and the local busybodies. The crime scene was quickly cordoned off with yellow tape and thoroughly searched until after dawn. Ultimately, they found very little — a Dairy Queen cup, a beer can, a Sprite bottle, some cigarette butts. But this was a picnic area, filled with such flotsam. The only tire marks at the scene were found to be old. There was, however, a "cardboard-like substance" on which the victim's body had lain and some black plastic that had fused into the skin from the heat of the fire. Everything was carefully gathered and marked as possible evidence by ISP Crime Scene Technician Paul Schuh.

Why Lake Lou Yaeger? The long, narrow lake — Lake Lou in local parlance — had been a favorite fishing, boating and necking spot for decades. Over the weekend, Litchfield and neighboring towns were abuzz with the story of the nude, headless, burning body found at the lake, named, incidentally, after one of town's more beloved mayors. It was the most sensational thing that'd happened in Litchfield since the Palm Sunday tornado of '85 carried off three of Charlie Rodewald's prize Holsteins. Sunday morning after church the jaws really flapped: Did you hear? Can you believe it? What's this world come to. A maniac like that on the loose.

Some kids who happened to be riding around in the park that night said they saw an orange-red cargo van with Missouri plates driving away from the scene. No one saw the driver or got the license number, but they all agreed that whoever was driving was sure acting strange, all drunked-up or something, cutting in front of cars, chasing some of them down Rollercoaster Road. But after that night, the van was nowhere to be found, as if it had been driven into the cornfields and vanished.

The nameless victim became known as Janie Doe and word was that she was local, that a prom dress and a corsage had been found near the lake. That story line could have ranked right up there with the best of urban legends, however it was pure fiction. In fact, the body was that of Lynne Darlene Matchem-Thomas, a 35-year-old St. Louis woman with a troubled history, who had been reported missing only two days earlier. By removing her head and burning her flesh, the killer had tried to make it so she would never be identified, and he nearly succeeded.

TWO

Seven miles east of Litchfield, on Illinois Route 16, lies Hillsboro, a bucolic town of 4,400. Hillsboro boasts a couple of attractions. It is home to Hillsboro Glass, the manufacturer of many fine silica products, including the brown glass for all Hiram Walker whiskey bottles. It is — or was — also the site of a middling-serious controversy involving a sign.

Hillsboro is the seat of Montgomery County, and, typical of most Midwestern county seats, its courthouse stands smack in the middle of the town square. Renovated in 1870, it is a stolid, red-brick edifice with a mansard roof and spearlike iron cresting along the roofline. Invariably, a war memorial sits on the court-house square. Statues of local patriots are popular. So are World War I caissons, shells of army tanks and gutted Air Force fighter jets. Outside the Montgomery County Courthouse a pitted, leaden Civil War cannon sits atop a concrete block, a bronze plaque bearing Lincoln's Gettysburg Address affixed to one side. Central Illinois didn't fly the Stars and Bars during the War Between The States.

Though the judicial offices and courtrooms have relocated, several county offices still operate in the old courthouse, listed on the state's Historic Register. The neon sign high on the facade of the old building reads, "The World Needs God." It is a bit odd that this message would adorn a county courthouse, as if to serve notice to scoundrels that salvation and jail time are one and the same. Local historians ascertain the sign was put up by a Sunday-school group, the Federated Women's Bible Class, around 1941, intended, some say, as a statement against a few bibulous town characters.

But time gathers romance around an object in public view, and though the sign has not been maintained in recent years — the neon ran out 30 years back — the townspeople generally like it, remembering the tubular letters that once suffused the square with a warm, red glow, comforting like some huge nightlight. Over in the gift shop of the Red Rooster Inn, they even sell porcelain coffee cups bearing a sketch of the court-house with a tiny "The World Needs God" sign that lights up when you pour in the hot coffee.

The ACLU chapter up in Chicago, however, saw the sign as neither nostalgic nor romantic, but rather as a blatant violation of the Establishment Clause of the First Amendment. On behalf of two anonymous county residents terribly offended by the sign's message, they filed suit in federal court for its removal. The towns-people were incensed. Some said the suit was a prelimi-nary action to remove "In God We Trust" from the currency. Others said it would be a sad day when the god-dam atheists get their way. State's Attorney Kathryn Dobrinic, based in Hillsboro, argued the case against the ACLU lawyers before U.S. District Judge Richard Mills. But no arguments, however well-crafted, could overrule the law of the land. You simply cannot have a public building extolling God. After 55 years of presiding over the town, the landmark was ordered taken down.

At first, there was a groundswell of support to fight the decision. The county board convened and voted to appeal the ruling. Yet, after Dobrinic advised that legal fees involved could mean a tax levy of up to $500,000, the board suddenly changed its collective mind, voting to end the appeal, prompting the headline in the Decatur paper the next day: "County Gives Up On God."

That hurt.

THREE

In a sort of slap in the face of their heritage, many counties have abandoned their nice, old courthouses for larger, modern facilities, typically some soul-less, boxlike edifice. Montgomery County was no exception. The county's new Justice Center, a courts-and-jail complex, sat just off the square, a minute's walk from the old courthouse. In the bowels of this steel-and-concrete citadel Curtis Thomas changed out of a prison orange jumpsuit into dress clothes, something he might wear to a cocktail party or an art gallery opening. The attire wasn't GQ, though it wasn't Kmart either.

First, the pressed white shirt, followed by the dark slacks, the charcoal-gray sport coat and tie. Curtis was about five-eight with a medium build on the muscular side. In jeans and a tank top he could pass for a laborer, a guy on a road crew or a roofer, wiry like that, but the fact was he hated physical labor, felt it was beneath him. At 38, he had short, thinning hair on a head that looked like a chunk of granite. The facial features were decidedly African-American — the wide nose, the full lips, the dark eyes, inquisitive, intelligent. If he looked at all unkempt, it was the beard he was attempting to cultivate, so sparse and patchy.

With a deft yank of the tie, Curtis executed a perfect Windsor knot. Unfortunately, there wasn't a mirror in his cell; he had to take the jailer's word that his appearance was neat and proper, certainly appropriate for the courtroom.

Curtis was ready for his trial. He had dreaded it for the longest time, ever since his arrest in late January 1995. But now, having been in the justice machine for nine long months, all of it behind bars, he was mentally prepared, almost eager, to get to the next chapter of the legal saga in which he was mired. Curtis Lee Thomas was charged with murdering and dumping the body of his wife of six years. That translated to two counts of first-degree murder and three counts of concealment of a homicidal death — hiding, burning and decapitation. The decap count, incidentally, alleged that he placed her head in a bucket of concrete.

It was now a week before Halloween, the 23rd of October. After several postponements, including a psychiatric examination to determine his competence to stand trial, Curtis was about to have the most celebrated time of his life. After seven days of trial, the strange events of the last two-and-a-half years would be intensely scrutinized in a court of law. At the trial's end, the way he saw it, he would walk out of the courtroom, dance a jig out front of the building, take in the glorious smell of burning leaves, maybe saunter over to Bob's Tap, the bar he'd seen when they hauled his ass

22

out of the cruiser and into this jail, order himself a Bud longneck, and then head back to St. Louis where his bon vivant life awaited. Or — *god no, please!* — he would be led back to his cell by one of those hulking marshalls who, after locking him in, would smile facetiously and walk off saying, "Have a nice day." And then he would sit there on his bunk, lower than an ankle bracelet on a flat-footed midget, banging the back of his head against the wall.

This trial was the crux of his checkered life and the outcome would rest largely on the legal acumen of Mr. Pat Conroy, a former St. Louis public defender now in private practice, and he, like Curtis, was a stranger in these here parts.

———•◆•———

Curtis Thomas had the distinction of being indicted by two grand juries, one in St. Louis and one in Montgomery County, Illinois. Missing were the turf struggles that can impede interstate criminal investigations. Indeed, this layered investigation was a highly cooperative effort between the Illinois State Police, the Montgomery County Sheriff's Office, the Montgomery County Coroner, the Homicide Unit of the St. Louis Metro Police Department, the Latent Fingerprint Division of the St. Louis Police Department, the St. Louis Circuit Attorney's Office and the FBI.

St. Louis held him first, but Montgomery County wanted him. After Curtis spent three months in city jail, the St. Louis Circuit Attorney's Office, by an order of *nolle prosequi*, voluntarily dismissed the case in order that Illinois handle it.

"It made sense," said Shirley Rogers, chief trial assistant under St. Louis Circuit Attorney Dee Joyce-Hayes. "All of the physical evidence was there as well as the witnesses and the investigators."

Indeed, ISP investigators, notably Special Agent Mike Sheeley and Inspector Richard Burwitz, had logged hundreds of man-hours on the case. The St. Louis prosecutors also may have thought he stood a better chance of being convicted in a county where murder is not an everyday occurrence.

Curtis cooperated and waived extradition. Handcuffed in the back of a squad car, he made the hour-and-a-half drive up I-55 to Hillsboro, a trip which Illinois state police inspectors and prosecutors were betting he had made once before — at least as far as Litchfield. They booked him into their nice new jail. In St. Louis, he had been held without bond; in Hillsboro, the bond was set at a half-million. He couldn't even pop for the 10 percent, $50,000 cash. He was not going anywhere.

A small-town jail must have been strange digs indeed for Curtis, a habitué of St. Louis' trendy West End with its private streets and sidewalk cafes. The product of 10 years' Catholic parochial education and a graduate of Washington University with a degree in language arts, Curtis was smooth, articulate and charming. He apparently made quite an impression on the good citizens of Hillsboro.

"Very early on," wrote *Montgomery County News* reporter Ron Leible in his *From File 13* column,

"Thomas became known throughout the courthouse as an outspoken brain, who, in pretrial hearings, was so disruptive in court he was nearly cited for contempt. But his rancor mellowed as the weeks wore on, and he became more and more ... well, likable."

Though Curtis could charm your socks off, "like-able" was a stretch. You don't *like* a caged porcupine with its quills ready to stick. And since they first saw him frogmarched from the police car to the jail, the townspeople regarded the prisoner with varying degrees of contempt. I met a man outside the Farm Bureau, said he was the deputy coroner of the county, and we were talking about the case.

"They got the one that done it," he informed. "The dead girl's husband."

"Yeah? What makes you say that he did it?"

"He's real manipulative. He's guilty as hell."

And this was before the trial even began.

FOUR

Locker number 32 held a pair of human hands. They had come into the possession of Gary Havey, a forensic scientist and latent fingerprint expert with the Illinois State Police Bureau of Forensic Science, Springfield. It was Monday, May 10, 1993.

Though crime scene technicians are trained in taking prints post-mortem in the field, in many instances it is more effective to remove the hands and bring them into the laboratory. If there are fine, exacting procedures to be done, removing the epidermal or dermal layers for example, it should be done in a controlled setting. Thus, the reason that Janie Doe's hands had been amputated by the pathologist at Springfield Memorial Medical Center earlier that day.

Officer Havey removed the hands from the brown paper bags they were in. He made a visual examination of both, noting some friction-ridge detail on the palms and to a lesser degree on the fingers. The fingers posed a problem. They were locked in a clutching gesture, bent in toward the palms. To get the best possible prints the fingers would have to be amputated. He set to work.

A latent print is one that is not readily visible, one which requires extraordinary means to make it visible. The most common means uses only fingerprint powder or ink, brush, lifting tape and a background to put it on. It's a method that had been perfected by Scotland Yard well over a century ago. Once the fingers were removed, Havey dusted the palms and fingers with a fine black powder. Then, using a specialized lifting tape, stickier than normal with no bubbles, he transferred the impressions onto a series of white print cards.

Most of the fingers had been burned severely, and yet the forensic scientist was able to classify them all. This classification was according to the Henry Fingerprint Classification System invented by Sir Edward Henry in 1895. The Henry system uses binary numbering to classify fingerprints based on three pattern types — loops, whorls and arches — and ridge counts.

Two digits of the decedent, however, the thumb and index finger of the left hand, were of such good quality that he was able to extract partial, suitable prints. This was far inferior to the ideal of ten complete, suitable prints, but mysteries have been solved with less to go on.

It took a half-day of painstaking procedure to get the standards on the two suitables. Cases such as this made Havey think about the future of body identification. Someday, he thought, they're going to take DNA samples from every newborn. It would be a small procedure, a microbiopsy, as simple as getting a vaccination, but doing it to everyone at birth would remove the stigma. The military was already starting to do that, DNA-typing. Fingerprints worked fine, but in battle sometimes you don't have any fingerprints left. Some day, mused Havey, they'll be able to encode your DNA on a microchip, put it under your skin or in a bone. The technology was already in place, right? Every product today has a UPC code, why not people? It would be a hell of a boon. Someone gets raped, you retrieve a semen sample, break it down genetically, search it through the computer — bingo! A match.

And when they start doing that, thought Havey, staring at the hands on the stainless-steel countertop, when they start cataloging people's indelible, individual genetic blueprints it'll be one step closer to the day of Big Brother, but at least we'll know in short order who these poor, nameless souls are.

Havey surveyed the magnified field, looking for any detail that might be used as a point of identification. Returning to his ruminations, he felt confident that fingerprinting would not become obsolete like the type-writer did in the '80s, not in his lifetime anyway. DNA-typing, you need an expensive laboratory, somebody with an M.S. in biochemistry, and it's not even portable. Fingerprinting, on the other hand, is very portable. With a tube of ink, a $180 magnifier and a piece of paper you can ID all sorts of people.

Once he had the the print standards, Havey ran them through the Automated Fingerprint Identification System. In the '70s, law enforcement spoke wistfully of computerizing fingerprints. With more and more police departments getting AFIS, that's done and gone. Some of these older ID guys will tell you that AFIS is the best piece of police equipment since the two-way radio. As a fingerprint finder, "it's like going from a musket to an automatic pistol," said one veteran.

When the latent examiner scans a fingerprint into AFIS, the program rapidly searches through a database of millions of individual prints, vastly reducing the time needed to search any one print. The system does not make the actual ID, but rather singles out file prints that closely match the print being searched. Once they get a "hit" with AFIS, the file card is pulled and the latent examiner makes a visual comparison, searching for minute similarities in the arcane and cryptic configurations. It is a job that requires more patience and concentration than finding Waldo in the department store.

But AFIS is only as good as its components. Missouri has its own database of a million 10-print files, with the larger departments — St. Louis and Kansas City — fiber-optically linked to the State Highway Patrol. Illinois has a similar operation, though it is not linked with neighboring Missouri. Each state — or in some cases, group of states — has its own AFIS database. By the year 2000, the whole thing will be more centralized and those departments that are linked-up will be able to print-search through the 15 to 20 million criminal files maintained by the FBI. But this was 1993, and Havey was not having much luck.

He had searched Janie Doe's partials in the Illinois AFIS, gotten only a few hits, and they didn't pan out. He then issued requests for AFIS searches from the adjoining states and eventually throughout all the state systems in the United States, Puerto Rico, and all the provinces of Canada. It was the most extensive AFIS search ever taken on by the department.

Even so, nothing was coming up and it was frustrating. That the prints were partials could be the reason. AFIS can search partial prints, but it searches them if they were chance impressions from a crime scene, significantly reducing the probability of a match. Another reason might be that Janie Doe a.k.a. Lynne Matchem-Thomas just wasn't in the system. AFIS, the prodigious search-engine of identities, is also only as good as its database. In this case, law enforcement was encouraged by the the fact that the preponderance of homicide victims — up to 99 percent in large, urban areas — have a criminal record, and therefore should be readily traceable. Counterbalancing this, however, was the fact that only about 15 percent of all Americans have been fingerprinted — for any number of reasons including criminal arrest — so the odds in favor of a positive ID on Janie Doe were not that good after all.

In fact, this last supposition was correct. Nothing resulted from the trace because Janie Doe's prints were not in the AFIS system. Still, law enforcement agencies were notified that partial prints of a Jane Doe were available for potential match-up, and over the months that the body remained unidentified, Havey was contacted repeatedly by other jurisdictions concerning various missing women from their bailiwicks. Whenever prints of the missing were available they were forwarded to Springfield, and Janie Doe's partials were compared to them. It was a tedious and frustrating task, even for a patient man like Gary Havey, but one by one the possibilities were eliminated.

FIVE

From the onset investigators were hobbled by the condition of the body. It was so badly burned that Dr. Travis Hindman, the pathologist at Springfield Memorial Medical Center, couldn't determine the blood type. Because there was no perceivable trauma to the body and because of the absence of a head, he could not say conclusively the cause of death. He could not even tell whether the decapitation caused the death — no slight inconvenience to the man who would be charged with her murder!

Then, another roadblock popped up, a wrong turn of sorts. Based on findings made by Mark Johnsey, an ISP Crime Scene Technician who also is qualified as a forensic anthropologist, Janie Doe was classified as a Caucasian. This was quite a miscalculation given that a head shot of Lynne in the paper at a much later date showed a woman with strong Afro-American features. To be fair, it may be noted that Lynne was light-complected and that the skull is the most important factor in determining race. Race, incidentally, is a cultural term, not a medical or scientific designation. Johnsey was emphatic about that on the witness stand.

There are very few board-certified forensic anthropologists in the country, and Johnsey was not among their ranks. There are, however, many such as the ISP officer who have been trained in the discipline and who are readily utilized in investigations involving unidentified bodies or their remains. Johnsey held a master's degree in anthropology. He lectured on the subject at Saint Louis University Medical School, and, though he worked out of ISP's Metro East Crime Lab in Fairview Heights, he would occasionally help out St. Louis County Medical Examiner Dr. Mary Case.

An almost routine instance of the forensic anthropologist's services might be the scenario where a dog drags an unusual bone into the backyard. Some curious person, the dog's owner perhaps, shows it to the police who turn it over to the medical examiner's office. The medical examiner calls in the forensic anthropologist to determine whether the bone is animal or human, whether it is ancient or contemporary, male or female. With any skill, the forensic anthropologist will furnish data on the decedent's age, race and body structure. They can be very, very helpful.

Concerning Janie Doe, Johnsey based his assessment on armpit hair and pubic hair. Both were straight, he said, not at all tight and kinky like that of the average African-American. As a crime scene technician, Johnsey had processed more than 500 homicide scenes, and because his beat is East St. Louis, he said, he has seen the body hair on literally hundreds of black people. The body hair on Janie Doe was "very indicative of a white person." That's why he made the call he did.

Forensic anthropology is hardly an exact science. Ballistics and fingerprinting, for example, are grounded in objective criteria. Bullet "A" can be proven to have been fired from gun Number One because rifling characteristics can be neatly compared on other bullets test-fired from gun Number One.

The forensic anthropologist would be lucky to have anything that tangible to work with. Instead, he or she tries to give the investigators a picture of what the charred body, the headless body or the skeletonized body once looked like. In a case such as this one, where the identity is in question, it is imperative the picture be as complete as possible. Saying, for instance, that the victim was 20 to 40 years old is too broad a sketch.

At least Johnsey pegged her age correctly. A series of measurements on Janie Doe's pubic synthesis scored a phase seven in a scoring system called the Todd Ten. Her age range, he confidently stated, was somewhere between 35 and 39.

Using another forensic formula, the Trotter Equation for white females, the victim was estimated to be five-four to five-six, 120 to 130 pounds. An external examination showed her to be a chronic nail-biter; the autopsy showed a uterus enlarged three to four times normal size because of multiple benign tumors. It was suggested that she was left-handed and that she had borne a child. Neither of these last two things were true.

Based on Johnsey's profile, state police put out a bulletin to the media. It was circulated in newspapers and on television throughout the region. It was put on a teletype and disseminated throughout the country. She might have been a local woman, a woman from a neighboring state or from four states away. No one had any idea. Her identity was a puzzle, a riddle, an enigma. A nagging question mark.

Yet, she had a name, a life. Someone somewhere was missing her. The answer lay in the murky world of missing persons.

SIX

Lynne Matchem-Thomas might never have been identified had it not been for the dogged determination of Detective Mike Sheeley, Special Agent for the Illinois State Police. A tall man in his mid-30s with short, straight brown hair and plain, metal-frame glasses, Sheeley has the pensive look of a history professor.

Sheeley had been the principal investigator from the very beginning. He dutifully followed every lead related to the Janie Doe case, looking into various unsolved decapitation murders as well as any outstanding missing person reports, some 500 throughout the country, on white and Oriental females. The names and identifying factors were in a thick file that never left his desk. Helen Lekousis W/F DOB 1/12/60 was adrift in this shadow world. So were Penny Prechtl W/F DOB 6/27/58, Rita Fouts W/F DOB 7/31/50, Camala D. Schuyler W/F DOB 7/8/63 and a host of others. It made Sheeley sad to think about it.

Sheeley had a stack of other cases to work on, but he never lost sight of Janie Doe, and it really bothered him that more than a year had gone by and nothing had shaken loose. Then Inspector Alva Busch entered the case. Inadvertently. Busch is an Illinois State Police homicide investigator, working out of the Metro East Crime Lab near St. Louis. He is a big fellow with a silver beard and steel-gray eyes behind the glasses. He went from a tour of Viet Nam — Army Airborne 1967-68 — straight into police work. A veteran of more than 500 murder investigations, he writes true crime books in his spare time. His literary style is straight-up-no-bullshit, just like his demeanor. Busch's boss is Mark Johnsey, the ISP investigator-anthropologist who misidentified Lynne Matchem-Thomas as a Caucasian.

One weekday in July, 1994, Busch had to go up to District 18 headquarters in Litchfield. His business there was on an unsolved murder, nothing related to Sheeley's quest, but investigators often confer informally on stumpers and Sheeley was at a wall with this one. In his office, Sheeley laid it out.

"I've got one," said Busch, responding to the scenario. "It's close to the time frame, but it's a black female." Sheeley shrugged his shoulders. At this point he was ready to accept anything. About that time Busch got paged. "Got to go," he told Sheeley, hanging up the phone. "Got a body in a bathtub over in Belleville." As he parted, they agreed that Busch would check into the missing woman they'd briefly discussed. Sheeley gave him a copy of the flier that had circulated about the van from the crime scene.

A couple of days later, Busch was in his office, shuffling papers, making phone calls. In front of him was the teletype regarding a black female, missing from St. Louis since May 5th of the previous year. There was no disposition on it. Busch knew that missing persons are sometimes returned and never taken off the list. The mother's name and number were on the report. What the hell, he thought.

Alva Busch identified himself to Shirley Matchem over the phone. "I don't mean to alarm you," he started. "I'm just working from a teletype, but ah ... has your daughter come home?"

Shirley Matchem was almost breathless. She missed Lynne immensely, and the not-knowing had hollowed her out. All these months, she'd been living on gratitude for the 35 years she had with her daughter. A couple of her daughter's friends held up the theory that Lynne had gone back to San Diego where she once worked, and was laying low, telling no one, not even her mother, where she was until she was sure that Curtis would leave her alone. Shirley, however, knew in her heart that couldn't be true.

"I'm sure she's dead," she told Busch plaintively. "She left her husband's house on her way over here and she's never been seen since. That was more'n a year ago."

Busch asked whether she was light or dark-complexioned. Shirley answered that she was light-complexioned. Chalk one, thought Busch. The next question could do it, but he didn't want to lead the mother by asking straight-out.

"Did she have any female problems, ma'am?"

"She was seeing a psychiatrist," Shirley Matchem answered.

"No, I mean was she seeing a doctor, a gynecolo-

37

gist?"

"Oh yeah," said Shirley. "She had tumors."

Sheeley was on the case, tracking a lead from Texas, when Alva Busch called. "Listen, I've got a hellacious lead for you. This has got to be your gal. Check it out."

SEVEN

In the year of our Lord 1993, the violent city of St. Louis racked up 267 homicides, about two murders every three days. The homicide rate in this city has markedly increased since the summer of '85 when crack cocaine was introduced by West Coast street gangs, the Bloods and the Crips. Since then, it has been a constant battle on the part of law enforcement to keep the grisly situation in check. Some days you wonder who is winning. Drive-by shootings are not uncommon nor is the sound of automatic gunfire in the not-too-far distance on a hot, summer night. Folks get shot standing on street corners waiting for the bus, sitting on their porches, walking to their car in the well-lit parking lot, sitting inside the McDonald's eating a bag of fries. You'd think it was the Wild West out there. Sometimes it's robbery, but more often it's retaliation; somebody did something to somebody at some time. Flashed the wrong gang signs, called some guy's girl a 'ho,' looked funny at some dude. All too often you read, "Police have no apparent motive in the killing."

There have been more than 2,000 murder victims in the city of St. Louis over the past decade. It is abhorrent and dehumanizing to everyone. Mostly, it is black-on-black crime, and that's a fact. The black community is painfully aware of this and so there have been many marches, prayer vigils and demonstrations to try to raise collective consciousness over the senselessness of the carnage. Dick Gregory, one-time comic turned nutritionist-guru and social activist, has led a loose-knit group, the Dignity Patrol, on several "Stop The Killings" marches. One of them passed down Waterman Avenue, right in front of Curtis' door.

However, Lynne Matchem-Thomas' murder would not be counted among the 267, for her corpse was found outside the jurisdiction and was not identified until well after the crime stats were published for that year. Her life and death is counted somewhere, though. If not by the states of Missouri or Illinois, then most certainly on the gilded pages of some metaphysical ledger.

On Wednesday, May 5, 1993, the last day she was seen alive, Lynne's brother, Jerome, was 10 minutes late in picking her up from Barnes Hospital. At 2 p.m. she had a one-hour session with her psychiatrist, Elliot Nelson. It was a nice day. Perhaps she felt like walking, thinking about her session. Not wanting to wait for Jerome, she left the rendezvous point at Barnes, heading home on foot. She was almost entirely moved out of the house she shared with Curtis and was living with her mother, Shirley. She may have taken a short-cut through Forest Park, so beautiful that time of year. She may have gone to visit Martin Plummer, her new boyfriend, living with his mother in their run-down, two-family flat on Cates Avenue. Whatever she did after 3 p.m. that day is unknown — until such time she reached the house on Waterman Avenue.

Lynne had reached the house at least by 6 p.m., for she and Curtis were out front talking when Deborah Claybrook drove up. A former girlfriend and renewed love interest, Claybrook had dropped by at Curtis' request, not expecting any third party. Yet, once she got out of the car she was immediately confronted by Lynne, who introduced herself as Curtis' "ex-wife."

Curtis muttered a curt hello to Deborah Claybrook, but that was about all. He wasn't making any eye contact with her. He seemed absorbed in this other woman, pretty and animated with a moderate 'fro — his ex or whatever she was. Claybrook felt awkward. She said something about coming back at another time and then she drove off in a huff; she wasn't going to be made a fool of.

Soon after Claybrook left, according to Curtis, Lynne set out west on Waterman, walking to her mother's house in the 6000 block of Washington Avenue, just three blocks up and two blocks over. A five-minute walk. She never arrived.

After a while Curtis called Shirley Matchem, asking for Lynne. She was not there. "She should be," said

No, that's not my daughter

Curtis, alarmed, "she left here 20 minutes ago."

The next day, around mid-morning, both Shirley Matchem and Curtis Thomas independently called police to report Lynne missing. She was initially classified as a "serious missing." Police took reports from both Shirley and Curtis. They conducted a door-to-door canvass of the neighborhood in the 5700 block of Waterman. From neighbors they learned that the couple had argued in front of the residence.

Where was Lynne? Her family was frantic. Curtis had seen her last, and they were sure he had something to do with it. Curtis, however, was not frantic. He didn't get emotional like that. But he was worried and he made his own investigation into the matter. He started by calling Martin Plummer and intimidating him with threats of physical harm.

Around 10 a.m. that Friday, May 7, Shirley Matchem and her niece stood outside the house on Waterman Avenue as St. Louis police officers Mike Priest and David Minor knocked at the door. Shirley had called the officers because earlier that day she thought she had seen her daughter on the third floor. She was crying, Shirley told them, crying and trying to escape. To the officers present, she painted her son-in-law as a rake and a Bluebeard.

Curtis answered the door and politely told the officers that Lynne did not live there and he hadn't seen her for a couple days. In fact, he himself had reported her missing the previous day.

"Could we come in and look around?" asked Officer Priest.

"Well, I'm entertaining," said Curtis haltingly.

"It'll just take a minute," replied Priest, "and it'll give the lady some peace of mind." He nodded toward Shirley, off in the shadows.

Curtis gazed at Shirley somewhat disinterestedly. "Well all right," he said, "come in and look around but please make it quick."

Shirley Matchem and her niece waited outside as Priest and Curtis talked in the foyer. Minor began to look around and soon found a woman in a room on the second floor. She cooperated fully when Minor asked her to step to the outside door to be identified. Shirley, standing on the walkway leading up to the porch, squinted at the near-silhouette. She shook her head sadly. "No, that's not my daughter," she said.

It was Deborah Claybrook.

A short time later, Officer Minor, still looking around, had his hand on the doorknob leading to the basement. He was starting down the steps when Curtis, cooperative until that moment, voiced protest.

This has gone far enough, he told the officers calmly but firmly. I'd like you to stop until I talk to my lawyer.

As they waited, Curtis called his friend, attorney Herman Jimerson, who dutifully told Curtis to inform the officers to stop the search and leave the premises. The officers had no warrant, and Curtis had given a verbal consent to the search; the officers had no choice but to comply.

At the area station, the officers told the district watch commander what had happened. Feeling that something was amiss, they asked for permission to prepare a search-warrant application. The watch commander said they did not have enough probable cause to do so, but that they should apprise the district detectives of the circumstances. Nothing came of it, however. A search warrant for the home on Waterman Avenue would not be issued for another 20 months.

———◆•◆•◆———

Independence Center runs several adult psychiatric rehabilitation facilities. Affiliated with Barnes-Jewish

Hospital, the Center provides an alternative for persons with serious and persistent mental illnesses who cycle in and out of hospitals, coming out better for the short-term perhaps, but in the long run not well enough to be able to integrate into normal workaday society.

Curtis was a resident assistant at the Center's Holtwood facility, in Olivette. The facility was a series of nondescript duplexes, semi-independent housing for the residents, with a community room at the hub. His job was to look in on these residents in their little apartments, make sure they were OK, see that they took their medications properly and so on. On Saturday, May 8, Curtis took the bus to work. Pulling an 11-to-9 shift, Curtis had the place much to himself because of a weekend staff retreat in Washington, Missouri. In fact, only Curtis and one other employee, Gloria Ann Jones, were on duty during the day shift; they overlapped from 4 til 9. Curtis and Jones worked in different parts of the facility, had different residents to attend to, and although she would encounter him from time to time, there were long periods when she didn't see Curtis at all. The day was quiet and uneventful. Curtis is supposed to have left work at or about 9 p.m., though no one could say for sure.

Here the story diverges. Curtis says he had arranged for a friend, Aaron Seymour, to pick him up. Aaron was late, but Curtis insists he did pick him up. They bought beer and went to Curtis' place to hang out until as late as 1 a.m. But no one saw Seymour arrive.

The prosecution's version contends Curtis took the keys to the Center's van and either drove home to get the body of his wife or somehow already had it at work. Regardless, he drove up Interstate 55 that evening with the intent of disposing of the evidence. Driving time from St. Louis to Litchfield, Illinois is about 70 minutes from Curtis' house; less time from Holtwood. The immolated body of Janie Doe was discovered, at best estimate, between 10:15 and 10:30 p.m. that night.

EIGHT

Maureen Powell padded in her slippers to the ringing phone. It was Sunday morning, May 9th, and she was mildly anxious in anticipation that it was her mother on the line, going to guilt-trip her for not calling to wish her a happy Mother's Day. Well, it's only 9:30, she would reply, assuaging any hurt feelings, I just now got up, Mom. I was going to call you as soon as I got some coffee. So, how's it going?

As it turned out, she needn't have been concerned about a jilted mother, for the phone call was from one of the residents at Holtwood, where she was a supervisor.

"Miz Powell," he started, "do you know where the red van is because I haven't seen it all weekend?"

Mo Powell was responsible for the use of the three vans owned by the Independence Center for the transportation of residents. The voice on the other end of the phone she knew as Tom Ryan, a Holtwood resident or "client" as they were called. Part of Ryan's rehabilitation duties involved caring for the vans — washing, cleaning the interior, minor maintenance. It was a job he undertook with great enthusiasm. He was understandably upset, Powell realized, and she tried to calm him.

"Well I've been at the staff retreat much of the weekend," she told Ryan. "It's possible that someone requested it after I left Friday afternoon. I won't know until I get in tomorrow morning and check the log. Let's wait 'til then and hope all's well."

That next morning, Monday, May 10th, Mo Powell and Nancy Anderson, a resident assistant, were sitting on the back stairs at Midland House, an administrative building just a block over from the Holtwood complex. They were debating whether to call police about the van. It was definitely missing. The last time either woman could remember seeing it was sometime the previous Friday, before they had left for the retreat. It had not been logged out since then, though that didn't necessarily mean it was stolen. They had to concede that as a record-keeping procedure, the van logs were less than comprehensive. They promised to be more diligent about it.

Suddenly, the van drove up and pulled into one of the parking spaces in the small asphalt lot. Curtis Thomas stepped out. The women sat there dumbly, expecting an explanation. But Curtis never even glanced at them, much less said anything. Instead, he strolled over to the sidestreet, got into a parked car and drove off.

"Can you believe that?" asked Anderson.

"That is the very definition of gall," said Powell.

They walked over to the van and saw that the keys were in the ignition. Everything else looked all right.

"Well, Mr. Ryan will be relieved to see this back," said Anderson.

"Did Curtis work yesterday?" asked Powell.

"He worked Lohmeyer, the day shift," answered Anderson. Lohmeyer was another Independence Center facility located in Maplewood, on the southwestern edge of the St. Louis city limits.

"Do you know when he works next?" asked Powell.

"He comes in at 9 tonight," answered Anderson. She was a sponge for all sorts of data, including the other R.A.'s work schedules.

"I think I'll write him a letter of reprimand," said Powell.

———————•◆•———————

The weeks dragged on and Lynne may as well have been in another galaxy; there was no sign of her. For awhile, the St. Louis police were looking at Martin Plummer, Lynne's new flame at the time of her disappearance. Plummer was somewhat of an enigma. For instance, what did he do for a living? He had no job, no visible means of support. He lived with his mother. Even the "read" on him was inconsistent: Herman Jimerson, Lynne's longtime friend, in conversation, referred to Plummer as "lower than a pimp," whereas Lynne's mother was more approving, describing him as "tall, handsome and gentle-mannered."

Curtis knew about Plummer's affections for Lynne. He had seen them together and it infuriated him. When she disappeared, Curtis either truly blamed Plummer for Lynne's perplexing eclipse or he wanted to give the impression that he did. He started a campaign to harrass Plummer by phone and on one occasion he picked the wrong time to threaten.

St. Louis detectives were at Plummer's house on Cates Avenue in the city's West End. It was the same street on which the novelist and screenwriter Fannie Hurst had once lived, and she would have blanched to see the state of disrepair the once-stately homes had lapsed into. They were grilling Plummer about Lynne. This was a routine action in all missing cases, interviewing those around the subject. Plummer, tall and lanky, tried to sink down into the living-room sofa as the detectives bombarded him with questions.

He met Lynne, he told them, at Club Mercedes in Midtown. About oh, two months before she disappeared. Yeah, they'd had something going. Last time he'd seen her? Couple days before she was last seen. May 3rd, maybe the 4th. Shit, he saw her almost every day just up until she ... look, they had a thing going, OK? Yeah, he knew she was married, but she'd left that asshole, moved back with her mother. Now the crazy motherfucker was calling here, this house, screaming through the phone lines, making threats. It was really pissing him off because if he wasn't home when Curtis called, his mother would answer the phone and she would get the abuse. It was her house, too. She didn't deserve that treatment, old and in delicate health.

As if on cue, the phone rang. Plummer answered and the detectives listened in as Curtis heaped choice epithets and imprecations on Plummer, the interloper who had thrust Curtis into a state of cuckoldry. The detectives rushed over to Waterman Avenue, six blocks away, and arrested Curtis for harassment. It was a misdemeanor that he wore like a badge of honor.

As long as Lynne remained missing no one was being charged with anything serious, such as murder. But that didn't mean the cops were impartial. If she turned up dead, they would be looking past Plummer to Curtis as the likeliest culprit. Cops will tell you the spouse is always an automatic suspect in these missing-gone-to-murder cases, yet the book on this spouse raised more than the usual red flags. For one, though Lynne had been spending the nights with Plummer, Curtis had reported her missing the morning after she was last seen. At his house the previous afternoon.

Further, the couple had a history of domestic violence. Only days before she disappeared a police report had been filed in connection with an incident at St. Mary's Hospital in the suburb of Richmond Heights in which Lynne claimed, and witnesses corroborated, that he, Curtis, punched her, bit her and threw her out of a moving car. The cops were aware of this, and for weeks after Lynne's disappearance, they were buzzing around Curtis. If they couldn't pin anything on him at least they were letting him feel some heat.

Detective Sgt. Tony Rice of the St. Louis police had a bad hunch about Curtis from the get-go. "People are very concerned when relatives and loved ones disappear," said Det. Rice, "but this guy, he would call to get a daily update. He called her mother every day too. I became suspicious of that. It seemed he was trying to find out what we knew."

Curtis' concern may have been real or consciously acted out to give the impression of concern; it didn't matter. Nothing was going to come down on him as long as her body, 70 miles away, remained unidentified.

NINE

Rebecca Bellan heard him. So did Tammy Smith, Beth Brown, Paula Yancey, Derek Liter, Judy Ravellette and several other co-workers. They were at the Hacienda Restaurant on Woodson Road, not far from Midland House. It was July 1, 1994, the occasion of Tyronne Robertson's going-away party. Curtis would miss Tyronne at work. Several times, Tyronne had given him a lift home after work. Curtis usually didn't have a car.

Curtis was the center of attention. With a half-circle of astonished co-workers listening on, he spoke animatedly of his criminal exploits — how he had robbed a restaurant years before, how that after the robbery he faked his own death and fled to Canada. For awhile, even his mother thought he was dead. He had been a real desperado, but he finally gave himself up and agreed to be extradited to St. Louis, he said, only

And oh, I didn't have anything to do with my wife's disappearance

because the police were trying to implicate another member of his family in the robbery.

Curtis was just warming up. Now he was talking about his missing wife, saying how he was going to file suit against Lynne's psychiatrist for not somehow restraining her. Someone in her condition should have been hospitalized, the woman staying out all hours, never knowing when she was coming home. Drinking on her medication, brawling, hallucinating. She was off the deep end, you know? Way over her head, and what did that shrink do? Give her more pills, that's what.

Talking about how the police had been to his house. Talking, talking. A little later, as Rebecca Bellan recalled, Curtis blurted out, "And oh, I didn't have anything to do with my wife's disappearance." But he may have said "death," not disappearance. Bellan couldn't recall, except that he punctuated this remark by crossing himself.

Lynne Matchem-Thomas had been missing for 14 months. Everyone who worked with Curtis was aware of this by now. Curtis had discussed the situation with almost everyone at work who would listen, including the patients, a verbal transgression for which he was reprimanded. His wife was manic-depressive, he volunteered. She sometimes ran with a fast crowd. She had wandered off in the past and it had likely happened again, only this time she was much further afield. Anyway, he had not given up hope; he was still trying to find her.

But this was a party and no one really wanted to hear about the melodrama that had become Curtis' life. Curtis, however, was drinking and becoming expansive, a recurring condition which tended to get him in trouble.

Bruno Sonnino, Curtis' immediate supervisor, had come to the party as well, and he was close enough now to the ebullient Curtis to hear him brag that he was being paid for working two jobs at once. While he was working for Independence Center, he was also working as a home-care aide for Blacks Assisting Blacks Against AIDS (BABAA). Both jobs had a lot of autonomy and required him to be in the field visiting clients, so accountability was not a problem. He brought out two pagers, one from each employer, and flashed them around. "See," he said, "you just float until somebody pages you." He was proud of himself for double-dipping.

Sonnino listened intently. So, he thought, the rumors were true. Curtis had been promoted to community support worker a few months before, and it was soon after that rumors about him holding multiple jobs began to surface. In his new position Curtis was to work two days a week at one of Independence Center's facilities, and for the remainder of the work week he was supposed to visit clients who had achieved sufficient skills to allow them an independent existence in their own apartments.

But Curtis hadn't been in his new position very long before the agency began to receive complaints from these quasi-independent clients alleging they rarely saw Curtis. Not only that, but Curtis was not showing up for meetings at the various facilities. Moreover, a subsequent review of patient progress notes submitted by Curtis contained several irregularities and painted a far different picture of his activities on behalf of the Independence Center. In short, he was screwing off on the job.

Now that Sonnino had caught wind of this malfeasance, he took the initiative to call Beverly Seals-Caradine, Curtis' supervisor at BABAA. They were both chagrined by the revelation that their trusted employee was charging the same time to both employers.

Curtis was fired from both jobs. Seals-Caradine would tell Agents Burwitz and Sheeley that Mr.

Thomas was let go for "failure to comply with management directives, claiming compensation for periods of time in which he failed to account for his activities and misappropriation of management services in that he engaged a housecleaning service provided by the agency to clean his own residence at company expense."

It was Curtis' wont to take advantage of any given situation. Sometimes he got over and sometimes he got caught out. Again and again, he demonstrated that when it came to loyalty and trustworthiness, his principles were as a pliable as a Gumby toy. The man would steal a dead fly from a blind spider. This trait was instinctual, I believe, a pattern of his nature that was in lockstep with both his extraordinary cunning and unabashed avarice.

TEN

When Mike Sheeley walked through the gray granite entrance of police headquarters on Clark Street in downtown St. Louis, he was optimistic. The feeling of futility might be at an end, he reflected. In his interview with Shirley Matchem he learned that Lynne had once worked as a private watchman in the city, and that led him to believe he was about to connect the dots between Janie Doe and this missing St. Louis woman.

Fingerprinting is required of all watchman-license applicants. Those prints were stored in this building.

"We've only got so many megabytes available, so we don't put our civilian files into the computer database," Officer John Vogan, supervisor of SLPD's Latent Fingerprint Unit, explained to Sheeley. Vogan had been a crime scene technician for 18 years; he had 27 years of fingerprinting to his credit, and he was one of two people in the department who was internationally certified as an expert on latent fingerprinting,

"Now, if she had a criminal record, AFIS would spit her right out. But watchman applicants, we're only checking to see if they have a criminal record. And all the cards, after we're through with them, are unclassified. They get filed here." Vogan tapped a large, motorized rotating file.

Vogan opened the top drawer. There were scads of watchman cards lined in rows, possibly several decade's worth. "They're filed by the date they were rolled," said Vogan. "Do you know when that was?"

"Her mother thinks Spring '92."

"Let's start with March then."

They flipped through the cards manually. Vogan remarked that he had never ID'd a missing person through the watchman files before. Sheeley said he hoped to hell this would be a first. This could take awhile, Vogan was saying, but 30 minutes later he got to the month of May, and Lynne's card appeared. They took it to the print glass with its 5X magnification and compared it to the print card of Janie Doe which Sheeley had brought along. It sure looked as though the prints on the left thumb and left index fingers were the same. Gary Havey would later confirm it.

"It's her! That's your victim," said Vogan to an excited Sheeley.

It was August 4, 1994, almost a year to the day that Janie Doe was buried in Cedar Ridge Cemetery, outside Litchfield.

The first time Mike Sheeley saw the house on

They broke the news to him that his wife had been gruesomely murdered.

Waterman Avenue, in the DeBaliviere neighborhood, he assessed it as a cop and a homeowner. It was a red-brick, three-story job, circa 1920, much like every other home on the tree-lined street, except this one had a cement porch. Just about all the houses in the city of St. Louis were brick, red brick, the color of fresh calves' liver. Unlike certain other parts of the city which had a desolate, bombed-out appearance, this neighborhood, with its retail shops and restaurants and MetroLink station nearby, was bustling and alive. One drawback to living in a neighborhood like this, thought Sheeley, was the claustrophobia. Open your window and there's your neighbor, right there. Some of the homes were so close together you could stand in the gangway between them, hold out your arms and touch two at once.

It was August 12, 1994. Sheeley and Sgt. Joe Nickerson, a veteran St. Louis homicide detective, had gone there to notify Curtis of his estranged wife's identification.

He answered the door. He did not invite them in. That was OK by the cops. They were mainly interested in his reaction. They broke the news to him that his wife had been gruesomely murdered. "He was real passive," Sheeley recalled, "almost like he was intrigued by it."

As the detectives were leaving, Curtis shook his head in disbelief — real or feigned. "This whole thing is like an Alfred Hitchcock movie," he said, though he didn't say which one.

ELEVEN

From that day on, they viewed Curtis as a suspect and he sensed it. For the next few weeks he and Mike Sheeley played a kind of cat-and-mouse game with Curtis calling the detective at District 18 in Litchfield, emoting distress and concern, even as Sheeley was actively building a case on him. He called the day after the detectives visited and again a few days later, asking for a certificate of death and a copy of the autopsy report on his wife. He asked to be apprised of any break in the case.

Sheeley invited Curtis up to Litchfield to see the gravesite. Curtis did not come. Sheeley also invited Shirley Matchem, and she had accepted, coming with her immediate family. Mike Sheeley personally took them to the cemetery, a picturesque place nestled in among a stand of old pines. It was, he felt, the least he could do to give the family closure to this horrible ordeal.

As long as Curtis was calling and sounding concerned, Sheeley began questioning him, not in the tone of a cop grilling a suspect but more as a colleague, as if they were seasoned investigators working to solve a baffling case.

"I'd like to talk to anyone who knew Lynne, and yourself," said Sheeley. "That would be a start." Curtis was cooperative, giving him plenty of names including Martin Plummer. "He's the one you really need to look into," said Curtis.

In fact, they *had* looked into him. With Lynne's body identified, St. Louis detectives once again sought to question Plummer, but he had left town soon after the first interrogation. By asking around, they tracked him to a homeless shelter in Richmond, California. They requisitioned Richmond law enforcement to question Plummer about the case, now elevated to a capital crime.

Whatever he said must have convinced the detectives that he was straight. "They interviewed him extensively," Mike Sheeley said in a subsequent interview, "and they all felt pretty good he wasn't the guy, so he was ruled out as a suspect."

Of course, he wasn't going to tell Curtis that. He was going to milk Curtis for details, hoping to somehow trip him up. Sheeley knew from the police report of May 7, 1993 that Curtis had a woman in his home. Maybe she could shed some light.

"What about the woman who was at your home that evening the police came by," asked Sheeley, "just after Lynne disappeared? Maybe she could be of help, if we could locate her ..."

"Oh right," said Curtis tentatively. "That's ah, Deborah. Claybanks ... Claypool? Something like that. I haven't seen her for a long time. I don't even know where she lives."

"About this van," pressed Sheeley, "the one placed at the crime scene, a reddish-orangish cargo van. An older model, may be a Ford. Do you know anyone who drives or has access to a vehicle like that?"

"No, not that I can think of," answered Curtis.

It wasn't long before their investigation proved him a liar. Though their romance was over, he was still in touch with Deborah Claybrook, and it didn't take more than a couple of phone calls to ascertain that Curtis had access, through his job at Independence Center, to a van fitting the description of the one leaving the fire scene. Of course, 15 months had passed from the murder to the investigation, ample time for thorough housekeeping on any bits of evidence — hair, bloodstains, tissue — that might have existed in the van or anywhere else.

Throughout the Fall of 1994, investigators in both Missouri and Illinois worked diligently, compiling a body of circumstantial evidence, a picture of culpability, intended to show convincingly that the estranged husband was good for the crime. The prosecutor's offices in both St. Louis and Montgomery County, Illinois, had Curtis in their sights. Each jurisdiction presented the case to a grand jury, whose job it is to decide whether there is enough evidence of wrongdoing to indict someone. If one jurisdiction wasn't going to indict, the other one was. In this case, both grand juries looked at the evidence and decided that Curtis Lee Thomas should be indicted for first-degree murder.

They came for him on a Tuesday, a cold day at the end of January. He was in between jobs and just idling around the house, thinking about pounding the pavement looking for work, or, better yet, get a roommate, someone professional. He had it all figured out. He would ask $350 a month for the rooms on the second floor, and with that he could make do with a part-time job. Part-time was good. At some time or another your lifestyle made you choose: more income or more free time. Of course, he wanted both, wealth *and* leisure, but if he *had* to pick one over the other it'd be more free time. At any rate, he would check with state social services later in the week, see if they had anything.

He heard the doorbell, a protracted buzz. Peering through the peephole, he saw a group of serious-looking white guys. God, not again. He opened the door a crack. If he had known that from that moment forward he would never be a free man, he might have put up a struggle or bolted out the door. As it was, Curtis was arrested without incident at his home by Mike Sheeley and three St. Louis homicide detectives. They drove him downtown, and they put his pawprints on a white card. They had him smile for the camera. They gave him a nice, new outfit. After they booked him, the detectives returned to his house with a search warrant. They took a lot of pictures. They tagged and removed a lot of stuff, none of it worth much evidentiary value except some clippings from the *St. Louis Post-Dispatch* found in the telephone table – clippings about the body in Litchfield.

TWELVE

The Thomases moved to St. Louis from Dumas, Arkansas, in 1956, the year Curtis was born. The family settled on Vernon Street, in St. Louis' far West End, living in modest circumstances. Zachary Thomas, Curtis' father, died when Curtis was barely out of diapers. The family relocated to the northwestern suburb of Pagedale. Without a husband, May Ruth Thomas raised six children on the salary of a maid. Go out to the affluent suburbs of west St. Louis County — Ladue, Frontenac, Town & Country — and you will see the common sight of middle-aged African-American women in white uniforms waiting at the bus stops. May Ruth was one of these, a housekeeper, a dayworker, a servant to the rich, white folks – a condition that surely made an impression on young Curtis.

Curtis attended St. Rose of Lima Grade School on the North Side and went on to Christian Brothers College, a top-ranked college preparatory school, which, at the time, 1970-71, had a strong ROTC program in place. The students wore uniforms that made them look a little like mailmen. They wore colored name tags according to their year — yellow for freshman, red for sophomore, et cetera. They had drill. They were taught by retired military officers as well as the stern Christian Brothers.

"And it was 'Yes, Brother. No, Brother.' Not 'Yeah,'" said Bryan Hagerty, a teacher and football coach who arrived at CBC about the time Curtis departed. "It was pretty much a no-nonsense education," according to Hagerty. "There was not much free time. If they misbehaved they got demerits, and those demerits had to be worked off after school. It was the sort of place that a kid was sent when the parents or parent or guardian felt they really needed some structure."

While one classmate attests that Curtis was sociable and well-liked at CBC, another remembers him as an angry-looking young man. Some say he had a bodyguard. Curtis Thomas transferred to a public high school in his sophomore year, but a decade of parochial school education, with its emphasis on language skills would serve to help him integrate effectively into a white-dominated business world. In fact, Curtis would sometimes joke that he was bilingual. In the cultural sense. With equal proficiency, he could converse fluidly with a recruiter from IBM at the campus Job Fair or bullshit with the brothers at the newsstand.

The population of St. Louis proper is about half Caucasian and half African-American, with the former living mostly on the South Side and the latter living predominantly on the North Side. Curtis lived in the geographic middle of all this, the Central Corridor, and his preferences seemed to reflect it. His friends, for example, were white and black in almost equal numbers. He liked NBA games, the Chicago Bulls, but he also liked hockey, and he rooted for the Pittsburgh Penguins. Musically too, he was somewhat of an anomaly. Call me culturally naive, but if I had to guess what an educated black man in his late-30s would be into, I would venture something smooth like The Commodores or The Delfonics, maybe some Teddy Pendergrass or some rap with a political edge, like NWA. But Curtis wasn't down with that, not one bit. His favorite band was The Rolling Stones. He said he liked them because they represented the decline of Western Civilization.

Curtis attended Washington University — Wash U — the Midwest's answer to the Ivy League schools of the East. Though he was there intermittently during the '80s, studying political science, the registrar's office has him listed as a 1992 grad with a B.A. in language arts. Already a thinker with a nascent world philosophy, college helped him blossom intellectually. He loved to discuss issues with anyone who would listen. His college classmates from the '80s remember him as a firebrand.

"He talked at campus parties that he was destined to become a leader," said Kevin Powers, who knew Curtis from both CBC and Wash U. "He was critical of Jesse Jackson and other black leaders. He thought he could do better."

"People knew his name at Wash U," said John Kukay, another associate. "Curtis was always an advocate for black rights, always stirring the pot."

Said longtime friend Rick Flynn, "He was a devout atheist, and his views on race were as radical as his views on religion. He didn't believe in interracial marriage."

As a young boy, Curtis would tell people that he wanted to be the president of the United States. At Wash U one year he ran for student body-president, and he almost won. It was an exhilarating experience; he was able to hone his rhetorical skills while at the same time attract a small following. He began to realize that he might play a significant role in the grand scheme of things.

In the mid-80s, Curtis became an entrepreneur, opening The Final Edition, a newsstand in the bustling Delmar Loop of University City, a popular mix of shops, bars and restaurants near Wash U. It later relocated to St. Louis Centre, downtown. The business was ideal for Curtis with his charm, social skills and yen for reading. "The Final Edition was a bright spot in the Loop," said Herman Jimerson, "a place of enlightenment, particularly for African-Americans."

Carol Crudden, owner of Ziezo, a boutique located a few doors down from the former Final Edition, remembers Curtis in the mid-80s as "fresh, full of life and highly energetic.

"I really liked being in his company because he had a lot of ideas and aspirations. He was always talking about how he was going to be rich and buy a mansion on Lindell with a three-car garage and a built-in pool," she said. "He was convincing, too. I always thought that one day he was going to get that house."

Carol and Curtis regularly attended meetings of the University City Small Business Association. "Curtis was very vocal at those meetings," Carol recalled. "His issues were usually racially motivated — blacks weren't being given enough incentive to open new businesses in the Loop, things like that — and he would get very self-righteous."

Though the business seemed to do well, Curtis decided to shut the doors in 1987 when the management at St. Louis Centre raised the cost of the lease. Curtis cast about for a new profession. He had already tried the real-estate business. What would he do now? It had to be something where he could use his head, his charm, his wiles. That was certain. Even his half-brother and co-partner in the newsstand, Bennie King, described him as "the intellectual type with a dislike for physical work."

So Curtis went to work for a series of social-welfare agencies. At various times he worked counseling juvenile offenders, assisting HIV-positive persons and finally, for Independence Center, as a resident assistant for adult psychiatric patients — all professions, incidentally, where he could be in positions of authority and, by extension, in control.

Though he gravitated to bureaucratic professions, he still aspired to entrepreneurism.

"I always knew him to be ambitious," said Dan Kelly, a friend of Curtis' since their early days at CBC. "He always dreamed big. I think he imagined himself as doing well and going far."

In the early '90s, said Kelly, Curtis "put together a reasonable plan for buying the defunct Ambassador Theatre downtown (St. Louis). He was going to turn it into a music venue, a nightclub. He really beat the bushes about that, talked to the SBA and several banks. It sounded like he had a half-million in financing lined up, but in the end he was something like

$50,000 short."

In 1991, Curtis worked briefly for *The Riverfront Times*, a St. Louis weekly with a free circulation of 100,000. Doing delivery, putting papers in the racks of the various outlets, he would confront the manager or any hireling who happened to be present, demanding to know how many blacks were on the payroll. This one-man affirmative-action program, ad hoc as it was, got him fired from the newspaper.

Never mind. He would get another job. He always did. There would be other opportunities to champion the downtrodden. Curtis was the Messiah, come to right all wrongs, even the score. So he thought.

THIRTEEN

Curtis' arrest did not catch everyone off-guard. Some apparently saw it coming and took secret delight in his downfall. "A lot of people took it for granted that Curtis did this, because they didn't like Curtis as a person," said Rick Flynn, "and this whole thing was gratifying to them."

Outside this circle of ill-wishers, friends and family were absolutely floored over the turn of events. What baffled them one and all was how someone who had as much going for him as did Curtis would be willing to jeopardize everything, especially his liberty, by doing what? Murdering his wife! They fought, sure. So do many couples, but Curtis would file for divorce before he would do some maniac thing like that.

Others who knew both Curtis and Lynne accepted that he may have killed her, but that it wasn't planned out. It just happened like a tree branch snapping in the wind. After all, they were at the crucible of their breakup. Maybe things just got crazy that day and he went off, taking domestic abuse to a new level.

And some took the news of what Curtis was accused of doing with anger or confusion, seeing it perhaps as an act of personal betrayal.

"I won't even consider that he did it," said Dan Kelly of his longtime friend, "because if he did ... it stuns to think I could be so totally wrong about a person."

"They never did no real investigation," said Bufus King of his half-brother. "Once they start focusing on you, you're screwed."

"He's a con man," said one old friend who asked to remain unidentified. "Once a con man always a con man, but they don't usually go to murder."

But the hardest hit by the arrest was May Ruth Thomas. "That took our mother real hard," said Bufus King. "It really stressed her out. Seemed like she just went down after that."

The St. Louis city jail, adjacent to City Hall, is a beautiful example of 19th-century stonework, though it's doubtful many of the prisoners appreciated that. Curtis had been cooling his heels there about four months before the Land of Lincoln called dibs on him. As if he were some sort of property to be exchanged.

Curtis' arrival in Hillsboro was quietly acknowledged by detectives Burwitz and Sheeley. The Illinois State Police investigators were quite busy in the spring and summer of 1995. Readying for the trial, they were probing everything and everybody associated with Curtis and Lynne Thomas.

On the morning of June 2, Burwitz drove into St. Louis. He went to the Independence Center administrative offices on West Pine Boulevard and served a subpoena to Executive Director Robert Harvey in order to obtain a copy of Curtis' insurance records. Harvey complied and referred Burwitz to Chris Clifford, the Center's personnel coordinator. The records were kept at Barnes Hospital, Clifford said. She would need a little time to pull them up.

Burwitz was back at District 18 in Litchfield when Clifford called around 2 p.m. What she had to say pleased him. Curtis and his wife had been enrolled in the health-insurance plan offered by the agency. He was paying a premium of $42 every two weeks, just under $1,000 a year. However, the documents on file at Barnes showed that Curtis Thomas cancelled his dependent wife's participation in the health insurance program sometime between May 6 and May 21, 1993, citing her disappearance as justification for the action. Clifford said that Curtis had attached a copy of a missing person-report to the form.

This wasn't the usual procedure, Clifford noted. If employees wanted to make any changes in their benefits — adding someone to their policy or taking someone off — they were to go through the personnel office. That was her job to initiate the change and forward it to Barnes. This was the first she knew of this. For some reason Curtis did an end run around her.

What about the life insurance, Burwitz asked. Curtis had taken out a policy after he became a full-time employee, Clifford answered. Though he was married, his mother was listed as the sole beneficiary.

Burwitz thanked her and put down the phone. He stroked his chin in thought. He stopped her benefits very soon after she was reported missing, possibly the same day! You don't just cancel someone's insurance like that, so soon after they're gone ... unless you think there's no chance they'll be turning up.

FOURTEEN

Burwitz and Sheeley were casting the big net over Curtis, interviewing his friends and relatives and then eliciting more names from them. The chain of intelligence stretched over at least four different states and involved dozens of people. One was Berry Relder, a handyman and Curtis' boyhood pal. Curtis had hired Relder to repair the west wall of his basement during the time Lynne disappeared. In a police interview, Relder said that he had worked in the basement the morning after the thwarted search attempt by Officers Priest and Minor. "There did not seem to be anything moved or disturbed," he commented. His tools and materials seemed to be just as he had left them.

Relder told the detectives that Curtis had enlisted his help in "cleaning out the basement a short time after Lynne was reported missing. The basement contained a large assortment of Lynne's belongings, including items of clothing."

That clothing, said Relder, was packed in cardboard boxes and black plastic bags.

In his statement, Relder also commented that during this time, the first week of May, 1993, Curtis showed him divorce papers that he had prepared himself. Curtis confided that the marriage was over. "Everything good about it is gone," Relder had him saying.

Curtis, said Relder, "complained how he had to do everything. He was constantly providing Lynne with finances to continue her education, and she did nothing in return." According to Relder, Curtis said that "Lynne had become a burden on him."

The Litchfield investigators also zeroed in on Curtis' co-workers at Independence Center. One of them was Luanne McPherson. A resident assistant, as was Curtis, McPherson worked for Independence Center during the critical period of the investigation, for 18 months beginning in October 1992. She told the detectives that one day as she and Curtis were sitting in the community room at Lohmeyer, one of the Center's three resident facilities, he told her that he had been "taken by police to Litchfield, Illinois to identify a body. That's all he said, 'to identify a body,' he didn't say whose body, and I didn't ask."

When was this, the detectives wondered. She couldn't put it into any specific time frame, but it had to be before May 1994 because that's when she left the Center for another job. Strange, the detectives mused, the body wasn't identified until August 1994.

McPherson, along with Mo Powell, Nancy Anderson and several other former co-workers, would end up testifying in court against him. Curtis loathed them, having caught wind of their betrayal, as it were, while in jail awaiting trial. Why were they doing this, he asked in letters to friends, fabricating all these lies?

He told me that he had been taken by police to Litchfield, Illinois to identify a body

Another co-worker was Vicki Wieselthier, interviewed by Inspector Burwitz in June 1995. She told Burwitz that in one or more subsequent conversations dating back to 1994 after the body was identified, Curtis "mentioned that his wife's family and police thought he might have killed Lynne." She said he also wanted "to hire a private detective, since police seemed not to take the matter seriously and chose instead to focus their efforts exclusively on him."

Wieselthier was a fountain of information, telling Burwitz that she was "fairly certain that during one of their talks Curtis stated, 'If I did do it, they'd never find out,' or words to that effect."

She also volunteered an assessment of Curtis' character, describing him as "a cold and calculating individual, one who felt he deserved the best and one who would not allow another to stand in the way of his getting it." He was arrogant, she went on, convinced that whatever he did was right and that rules didn't apply to him.

The inspector had given Wieselthier a sanction to gossip and she was on a roll now. At one point, she continued, rumors sprouted that Curtis was stealing things from patients, and, as a result, staff members began playing a game with him. At Holtwood, where they worked, staff members had access to the closet, a locked area where valuables and keys to the vans were kept. She said that staff members who worked the shift before Curtis' would leave small amounts of coins or bills in a drawer in the closet, then notify Curtis' relief worker of the amount left and its location. Wieselthier claimed that in each instance, after Curtis had left and the relief worker checked the closet, the money was gone.

Sounds like a game called entrapment.

Some co-workers, however, had moved on. Inspector Burwitz initiated the out-of-state interview of one William Wayne Wertz, a former resident assistant with Independence Center. The request went west, falling to Det. Sgt. Tom Green, a local constable, who interviewed Wertz at his home in Butte, Montana in June 1995.

After establishing that Wertz worked with Curtis during the time that his wife was presumed missing, Green asked: "How did he get along with these people (clients) at the Center? Did he become violent with them?"

"No," said Wertz. "He was one of the most low-key, calmed-out-sounding people I've ever heard. If anything, he was just so quiet and even-voiced that he just seemed so mellow and able to deal with things. But at the same time he came across as a very intense person. He had very strong opinions about things."

Det. Green continued asking leading questions, trying to get Wertz to say that Curtis was a psycho, and when he couldn't elicit that he tried another tack. "Do you ever remember Mr. Thomas making any statements about his wife's disappearance or what may have happened to her?"

Wertz wagged his head emphatically. "No, to the point of it seeming funny because the guy's wife was ... disappeared and every now and then one of us would say to him, 'Have you heard anything? Do you have any idea?' And he was just so offhand like, 'No, I have no idea.' It might as well have been, 'Your dog's run off for five days. Where might it be?' And when anyone asked him about the circumstances of his wife being gone, he was just so calm and matter of fact, to the point of making us kind of raise our eyebrows."

———◆·◆·◆———

Curtis, meanwhile, was settling in to his role as a prisoner awaiting trial. By May, he was strapped on the justice conveyor, bumping along the various stations with their complex legal machinery, inching steadily toward a terminus. Once or twice a day, while being moved from place to place within the jail, he would catch a glimpse of the tree-lined streets of Hillsboro. He pined to be outside, strolling along, heading wherever he damn well pleased. The jail library, if you could call a small room crammed with outdated reading material donated by the Montgomery County Jaycees a library, afforded the best view of the town. It was there that Curtis spent as much time as allowed, poring over legal statutes, filing several motions on his own behalf. They all started out the same, in that loopy handwriting: "Comes now the defendant, Curtis Thomas ..."

One of his early attempts was a motion to dismiss charges on the grounds that his constitutional right to a speedy trial had been denied. Illinois law required a defendant to be tried within 120 days from the time of the arrest. To extend over that period, it was like picking a Get Out Of Jail Free card in Monopoly. This was June. Curtis counted 153 days since his arrest, the big question being whether his jail time in St. Louis counted toward this 120-day ceiling. His hopes were kindled as he awaited word on the motion. What a coup that would be, he mused, to get the judge to throw out his case because of a screwup on the part of the system. He could hear the judge now, some stodgy old coot with a voice like God: "It is a prosecutor's duty to watch her case, to make sure it goes to trial on time. Large blocks of time have passed without any forward movement in this issue. So, regardless of what I may think, Mr. Thomas must be freed ..."

But Circuit Judge Dennis Huber snuffed his candle. The incarceration in Missouri did not count toward the

120 days. In fact, Curtis would be jailed about 180 days in Illinois before he went to trial. The delay, however, was because of defense motions.

Curtis hired Pat Conroy, the former St. Louis public defender gone to private practice, soon after he arrived in Hillsboro, because Conroy filed a flurry of motions in late Spring 1995. One of the first things Pat Conroy did for Curtis was to petition for a change of venue, because, like some zombie that wandered in from the graveyard, Curtis' loathsome presence was causing panic.

" ... the defendant has received much unfavorable publicity in the County of Montgomery," reads the Motion for Change of Venue filed in May 1995, " ... too many to list. These various printed and oral statements have penetrated into the minds of the people of the county to such an extent that it is possible that a state of mass hysteria upon the part of the public has been created against the defendant."

Oh, how they must have hoped for Chicago. Instead, the motion was denied. It was a demoralizing blow. Curtis would be tried in the hinterland — Montgomery County, Illinois.

PART II

FIFTEEN

The trial began almost as sensationally as the crime itself: Minutes before the jury selection began, the two counts of first-degree murder against Curtis Thomas were dropped because of contention over where the killing occurred. Illinois law allows a prosecutor to file a murder charge in a county where a body is found, but the case will be marred if the state cannot show the murder occurred in that county. Jurisdiction is an element of the crime and the U.S. Supreme Court says all elements of the crime must be proved beyond a doubt, or the defendant walks.

In short, if you charge someone with murder in Montgomery County you had damn well better be able to prove that murder happened in Montgomery County.

In this case, Deborah Claybrook, Thomas' former love interest-turned-State's witness was planning to testify that he, Curtis, privately confessed to her of killing his wife in St. Louis and hiding the body in his basement for two days. When Patrick Conroy learned of this, he filed a motion to dismiss for lack of jurisdiction. Though Judge Dennis Huber ruled against the motion, Dobrinic voluntarily dismissed the charges. Why?

One theory says she might have thought that the judge made a mistake in his ruling, in which case a conviction would likely get overturned on appeal. From a more practical standpoint, she likely felt that an Illinois jury would not convict on murder when the evidence from the State is that the murder was committed 70 miles away in Missouri.

"It was never the State's theory that Lynne Thomas was killed in Montgomery County," an obviously crestfallen Kathryn Dobrinic told reporters. Yet, the state of Illinois extradited Curtis away from the proper jurisdiction, welcomed him with open arms. If this was to be the upshot of the exhaustive investigative work done by law enforcement to prepare for this trial, then why bring the charges to begin with?

The answer, according to Conroy, is that Dobrinic did not expect the jurisdiction to be challenged. "She got caught with her pants down," said Conroy of Madame Prosecutor. "She brought charges when she shouldn't have brought charges."

The St. Louis Circuit Attorney's office was not at all pleased either. Shirley Rogers, the chief trial assistant, called the development quite regretful, though she contended that no one could have foreseen it. "The law is not that clear-cut," she offered. "That's why we have judges paid to decide such things."

Clearly, filing that motion, setting up jurisdictional

haggling as he did, was the best thing Conroy ever did for his client.

The State's big gun had misfired. Left were three counts of concealing a homicide, a Class 3 felony, punishable by a maximum of five years. Dobrinic's task was now to prove that Curtis Thomas had taken steps to hide his wife's murdered body.

If Curtis had been despondent all those months in jail, he was back to his grandiose old self at the news that murder charges had been dropped. "I've already won," he said during a jury break that first day, "because the most I can get on this charge is five calendars."

He was already using the prison term for "years."

SIXTEEN

The etymology of voir dire stems from Old French — *voir*, meaning "truth" and *dire*, meaning "say" — and translates quite literally to "speak the truth." It refers to the process of jury selection, the questioning that opposing counsel put to prospective jurors, who, if chosen, are expected to fully and fairly listen to the facts on behalf of the State and the accused.

Attorneys familiar with the process have said that it's a little like getting to know the partners on your dance card.

Voir dire focuses on backgrounds and experiences of the prospective jurors or veniremen, as they are sometimes called, which may reflect on their abilities to be fair and impartial. If it's a criminal case, attorneys may want to know their feelings on firearms, say, or on the legalization of recreational drugs. They may ask if anyone has been the victim of a crime or knows anyone who has been. The object is to identify those who are likely to swing your way when closing arguments are finished.

Anybody who has sat through voir dire will tell you it often takes all day and can be boring as a room full of rocks – except to the defendant, whose liberty rests in the hands of these 12 chosen people. To the one on trial it's utterly riveting, the selection of average ordinary folks imbued with the power to exonerate or condemn.

In voir dire, counsel is provided with name, address, age, race, level of education, occupation and spouse's occupation of each citizen on the panel. Counselors may study the jurors' cards and make assumptions about them, but to truly ascertain whether they are going to hurt or help their client, they have to talk to them.

"The only way to pick the jury you want is to get to know them," says Jon Isbell, a former associate circuit judge in Madison County, Illinois. "That means unfettered voir dire. The more time you have, the more they volunteer of themselves. Looking at them, listening to them speak, you pick up on their intelligence, their socioeconomic circumstances — things which, when factored together, tell who will be able to identify with your client."

As with a board game, there are all sorts of rules. Attorneys get so many strikes for cause: "Mr. Jones has to go, your honor, because his brother was mauled by ferrets and the defendant has a pet store that sells ferrets." Then they get so many peremptory strikes, that is, the attorney doesn't like someone's look — he's gone. The attorney doesn't need to give a reason.

Well, not anymore. Since the landmark Batson case, the courts have ruled that people cannot be struck for their race or gender. Now, when a peremptory strike is challenged, counsel must show that it was unrelated to minority status. However, attorneys get around this by being cagey and citing reasons to strike that don't go to racial-gender bias: "She was glaring at me," or "I didn't like his response to the death-penalty query."

A good attorney, especially one who has lost a few cases because of an ill-picked jury, never underestimates the value of voir dire. In fact, some cases are won right there on the first day, during jury selection. There's a story about Richard "Racehorse" Haynes, the colorful defense lawyer from Texas. In the 1970s, Haynes defended a cop accused of shooting a Mexican who had attempted an illegal entry into the country. Having the venue moved from Southern Texas to the Panhandle, a place with fewer minorities, didn't hurt Haynes' chances for a not-guilty verdict.

Sometime later, on *60 Minutes*, Mike Wallace asked Haynes when he knew his client was going to be acquitted. Racehorse Haynes smiled and said, "When the last redneck was sworn in to that jury."

SEVENTEEN

In Judge Dennis Huber's courtroom, Kathryn Dobrinic, conducting jury selection in a gray button-down suit was oh-so chummy in her approach, winning over the panel of jurors with homespun charm and light banter. Dobrinic had won three or four death-penalty cases and was "right up there with the big boys," as one local attorney put it. But here on the home court — her office was just down the hall — she eased into her role like slipping into an old pair of sneakers. In a rural community where kinships are tightly bound, she was "jus' folks," a circumstance she certainly played up.

"What football team do you follow? The Rams? They didn't do too well yesterday, did they? Oh well."

And later to the same guy: "What are your hobbies? Do you like to hunt? Do you use a dog? Oh, what kind of dog?"

It seemed she was going hunting and was looking to borrow a pair of beagles.

At times, the small talk was downright ingratiating: "Well, Mr. Adams, I see you're from Raymond and you belong to the KCs there. Do they have enough money yet to build their new hall?"

"We're working on it," said Adams, warming to the question. "I think we have $75,000, a little over. We'll get there. We've got that fish fry coming up."

It was maddening. Why didn't Judge Huber intervene: Ms. Dobrinic, just what does all this chitchat have to do with the damn trial?

Pat Conroy, in his approach, was an entirely different animal. You might wonder whether he had ever heard the saying that you catch more flies with honey than with vinegar. His m.o. was to baffle or badger the jurors — and later the witnesses — by repeating variations of the same questions they had already answered. He was confrontative when there was no need to be.

Conroy to prospective juror: "If you have unanswered questions at the end of the trial and they create a reasonable doubt in your mind, what would your verdict be?"

Juror, slightly befuddled: "If there is reasonable doubt it would have to be not guilty." But the juror, clad in a Western shirt, quailed under Conroy's intense demeanor.

Conroy: "Right. Why did you look away just now? When you said that, you looked away from me."

Juror, defensive: "Well, because there's so many questions this morning ... it seems like it's asked one way from one side and another way from the other side, and I'm trying to decide if you are saying the opposite things or if you are saying the same things."

Of course, it's possible that Conroy was deliberately trying to rattle the poor fellow; he didn't want him on the jury, so becoming testy with him was a preliminary to dismissal.

Curtis would probably have been better off hiring a local attorney, ideally one as seemingly popular as Kathryn Dobrinic. Conroy had to be frustrated knowing that he was up against the poster girl of civic spirit. If you squinted hard enough, you could make out a faint halo around her head.

In his voir dire, as Conroy probed a prospective juror to see where his loyalties lay, he asked about Dobrinic's successful run for office:

"Did you contribute to her campaign?"

"I voted for her."

"Other than that is there anything you know about her which would affect your duty?"

The fellow pondered this for a second. "I've seen her at things up where I live. She comes to the festivals, and when we had a troop march for the soldiers — Desert Storm, you know — she was there. She's a morale-builder, I guess you'd say."

Conroy was also unfamiliar with certain aspects of Illinois law, for instance, telling the jurors that they were not allowed to take notes, which was not true. But more important, Conroy was perceived as a variety of bully who badgered witnesses unmercifully. Jurors promise not to prejudge, to decide a verdict based solely on the facts, but they are human and therefore subject to bias, however subtle or inscrutable. If they take a dislike to the attorney, it can rub off on the defendant.

Dobrinic, conversely, was the very model of concern for the juror's welfare. The hardship issue was mildly entertaining.

Dobrinic: "Mr. Johnson, you farm?"

Johnson says he does.

"Livestock or grain?'"

"Just grain."

"And what are you doing this time of year?"

"Tilling the soil, putting the fertilizer in it."

"This trial may go into next week. If picked, would that cause a hardship on you as far as your farming operation?"

"A little bit," concedes Johnson. "I'm not done tilling yet."

"Are there other family members to help out in case you're picked for jury duty?"

"The wife, I reckon, but she wouldn't like it none."

A chorus of chuckles emanated from the jury pool as Curtis looked to the ceiling, shaking his head in dismay.

The state's attorney wanted to know whether they work jigsaw puzzles, because the elements in this case would fit together like one big jigsaw puzzle. She wanted to know whether they think they have common sense because that is what they would need to grasp the big picture of Curtis' nefarious plan. Finally, she wanted to know which TV shows they watch. Did they ever watch LA Law? Do they watch courtroom TV? Did they watch the Simpson trial?

"TV is different," she opined. "That's for entertainment. What you see here in the court, this is real life."

The infamous O.J. verdict had come down earlier that month, and Dobrinic tried to impress upon the jurors that the legal machinations allowed in Judge Ito's courtroom would never fly in Judge Huber's courtroom. There would be no attempts to introduce irrelevant material, no calling of experts to contradict the testimony of a previous expert who contradicted the testimony of the first expert.

Judge Huber might have added his own caveat, directed at both Dobrinic and Conroy, that he would not tolerate attorneys who snipe at each other during session or who engage in rambling arguments.

The State had no smoking gun, as it were, only the word of a woman whose mental condition was at issue throughout the trial. Therefore, Dobrinic stressed the validity of circumstantial evidence. The layperson's view, she said, seemed to regard eyewitness testimony as irrefutable, but, in fact, witnesses sometimes lie, forget and interpret events to suit their own agendas. And despite being played down as something less in television shows from *Perry Mason* to *Law & Order*, circumstantial evidence doesn't lie. It offers important facts and findings from which jurors can draw the right conclusions. She wanted her jury to regard it with the utmost gravity.

"If the judge tells you to consider circumstantial evidence, will you do that?"

Prospective juror: "Yes."

"In fact, will you follow all the judge's instructions, even though you might disagree with them?"

"Yes, ma'am."

"Even though they might disagree with Judge Ito's law in California?"

"Yes, ma'am."

As with O.J. Simpson, the case against Curtis Thomas was built on circumstantial evidence. But unlike Simpson, a black man in a big-city courtroom with a racially mixed jury, the defendant here was a black man, urbane and erudite, with an all-white country jury. If he did do it, and if racial solidarity would be even a slight factor in the verdict, Curtis Thomas could hardly have picked a worse venue in which to be tried; the populace of Montgomery County is as white as the Bunny Bread on the shelves of the local IGA. Even with jury duty determined by lottery, there was not one nonwhite person among the panel of 50 veniremen.

EIGHTEEN

During a trial, the courtroom generally divides in half. Those who sympathize with the defendant sit on one side, and those who want the defendant to crash and burn sit on the other side. It's a little like chapel seating for a wedding. Newspaper writers and sundry media bozos who are supposed to be objective sit in any pew which happens to be available. Curtis didn't have anyone in the courtroom, no apparent family and friends there for moral support. It was kind of sad. You'd see only the back of his balding head for the longest time, and then, after awhile, he would turn and scan the room, looking for someone he knew. Someone friendly.

I was neither friendly nor hostile. I was merely taking notes in the back of the courtroom, thinking about how mortifying it must be to stand trial for murder, to have the sordid details of your marriage and life laid out before a gallery of strangers. Curtis recognized me and motioned me over to his table. I went.

It was day one of the trial. Jim Vazzi, the portly sheriff of Montgomery County, sat next to Curtis, chewing a toothpick. "How do you like this Mayberry setup?" Curtis asked, nodding toward the empty jury box. They were outside on break, smoking and chatting in front of the courthouse. I replied that one juror did look a little like Floyd the barber.

We talked for a minute. Curtis seemed upbeat, even confident. Was anyone else coming up? Was I writing a story? When would it be out? Would I send him a copy? He assured me that the State's key witness was out of her mind and that she was out to get him. This whole trial was a plot to get him, but he would beat the rap somehow. The jurors worried him, however. I could tell. His tone when uttering that Mayberry comment was scornful and implied the jurors were bumpkins and hayseeds bent on railroading him.

Of course, it's natural to be disdainful of any group possessing the authority to sit in judgment of you.

One thing for sure, they were a stoic bunch, hard to read. It was anyone's guess what they really thought about this man accused of tainting their nice recreation area with a mutilated corpse, scaring the children, getting things all stirred up.

But then, Curtis Thomas had a history of stirring things up.

———— •◆• ————

On September 22, 1973, Curtis Thomas then 17,

was the inside man for an armed robbery. The Leather Bottle was a bar-restaurant on Forsyth Avenue in Clayton, a tony St. Louis suburb. Working as a dishwasher, Curtis let a gang of thugs in the back door.

George W. Linhares was the manager at the time. "I was sitting in the office on the phone talking to somebody when I felt something cold on my ear," said Linhares, recalling the incident 23 years later.

"There were five of them, young," he continued. "'Hang up the phone and open the safe,' they said, but the safe was the kind that needs two separate keys. I tried to open it but I was so nervous I fumbled with the keys a bit and they kept hitting me in the back with a pipe. One of them said, 'Shoot him!' And somebody else said, 'No, don't.'"

Finally, said Linhares, they got the safe open and took the money, a reported $1,600, which was never recovered. Meanwhile, a bartender and a waitress had walked in. The bandits locked them all in the storeroom upstairs, including Curtis.

"He played it straight in there," said Linhares of Curtis, "acted like he was as scared as the rest of us. I found out later from the police that he was the one who let them in. He was new on the job. I figure he came there to set us up."

The robbers were caught the next day. One of the guys ratted Curtis out and he, too, was arrested. In his arraignment, Curtis was charged with a count of first-degree robbery with a dangerous and deadly weapon — two .38-caliber pistols and a bludgeon, the lead pipe.

Curtis made bond, pleaded not guilty, and promptly skipped to Canada. En route, in Detroit, he is supposed to have faked his own death by throwing his clothes and wallet into the Detroit River and leaving a suicide note to his mother on the bridge above. This is a well-known story surrounding Curtis, part of his mythology, which he enthusiastically promulgated over time. He even had varying versions of the escapade. Another account has him placing his ID bracelet on a dead Haitian. Either way, it is certain he ended up in Toronto.

No one knows for sure how long Curtis lived in Canada, a few years at least. It might have been a decade if he hadn't gotten pinched on welfare fraud, cops and lawyers in two countries doing a tug-of-war over his butt. He was finally extradited back to St. Louis. There, three years after the fact, he pleaded guilty to the robbery. Lucky for Curtis he was low on the criminal food chain with no extensive record to plague him. He was given a suspended imposition of sentence: five years probation, successfully completed.

NINETEEN

Curtis liked to blab. That may have been his downfall. He blabbed at Tyronne Robinson's going-away party. He blabbed to co-workers at Independence Center. He allegedly blabbed to Deborah Claybrook, whose testimony would put him behind bars, and he blabbed to several little birds. In the South, when someone wants to dish out dirt on somebody, and they want to be discreet about their source, they say, "Well, you know a little bird told me that Missy Upshaw is in a family way, blah, blah, blah ..."

Curtis had a flock of little birds around him. One of them told me how he and Curtis stole a $12,000 Persian rug from Bixby Hall on the Washington University campus. While a student, Curtis had had his eye on it for some time, and to take it required only the backing up of a van to a side entrance on a snowy winter night and, making sure no security guards were about, lugging the thing down the stairs from the second floor. The university regents were damn angry about that, said the little bird; they really liked that rug.

They stashed the thing at Curtis' where it graced his bedroom, made him feel like a regular sheik, until he got a local antiques dealer to place it at auction with Sotheby's in New York. The little bird allowed that he was still sore at the way he was cut out of the proceeds from that sale.

Another little bird is now an emergency-room physician at St. Mary's Hospital in St. Louis, but in 1980, as a student, he worked in a warehouse along with Curtis. They ended up sharing an apartment for a short time. Here is what that little bird said: "As soon as we moved in, I started hearing all these stories from him. He said he led a gang in high school that robbed restaurant takes, you know, managers taking night deposits to the bank, but that he got caught and had to leave town."

Little bird No. 2 told how Curtis regaled him with his adventures on the lam. "In Toronto, he said he got in York University, and there he met a mentor who showed him how to work schemes like getting names off tombstones, roughly the same age as him, and somehow he would establish identities and collect welfare, or whatever they call the dole up there. Oh, and he talked about how he had worked his way into this well-to-do household, kind of like the son of Sidney Poitier-impostor in *Six Degrees of Separation*. But he didn't like the cat, so he set the cat up — those were his words. 'How'd you do that?' I asked. He said, 'I poured water on the carpet and claimed the cat peed there.'"

The second little bird soon moved out when he saw what Curtis was about — selling pot, double-dealing and screwing people over. Once, when the little bird came home, Curtis and his pals were sitting at the kitchen table, a pungent cloud of reefer smoke over their heads, a few dozen baggies on the table stuffed with product. Another time, when they needed stereo equipment, Curtis suggested they go to some high-end outlet where he could buy a top-of-the-line system for just $20 and a promise to pay the rest on credit.

"As we were driving off with this huge stereo, he said, 'Well, Curtis will never make another payment on this.' One of his distinctions was that he referred to himself in the third person, a very egocentric sort of mannerism. So I was curious, and I asked why wouldn't he ever make another payment, and he said that as long as you make one legitimate payment they can't prosecute you for the rest. That's the way he thought.

"Curtis," said little bird No. 2, "liked to brag about how smart he was, how he shafted the system, out-smarted the cops, ripped off a business. But he always figured he was ahead of the game and nobody could bring him down for anything."

TWENTY

It was the week before Halloween in Hillsboro, a bucolic setting an hour south of Springfield. Black and orange crepe decked the Main Street storefronts. Cardboard cutouts of cute little witches and spooks were taped to the windows. Cars drove by with hand-lettered signs on the rear windows: "Lady Hilltoppers - No. 1!" The high-school girls' volleyball team had just won the 1995 Carlinville Sectional Tournament. At Bob's Tap at the east end of the square, the regulars, munching peanuts and sipping cool Miller schooners, stared out the window at a gorgeous afternoon that only the Midwest could produce. Indian summer was having its last hurrah.

In Courtroom No. 2, Kathryn Dobrinic addressed the expectant jury:

" ... Shirley Matchem is also going to testify that she was concerned about her daughter, so worried that on May 7th, 1993, after 10 p.m. she called the police and she went with the police to the defendant's house on

Waterman Street, and the reason they went there is because Shirley was afraid her daughter was there and being held against her will or the subject of foul play. And you are going to ..."

At this point Conroy objected, just as he had been objecting throughout Dobrinic's oration. He asked to approach the bench; they approached. Conroy addressed Judge Huber, "Judge, defense is moving *in limine* to keep the State from mentioning any information from either Officer Minor or his partner that the defendant would not allow them to search his basement when they came to his home that night. That violates his Fifth Amendment rights, his right to search and seizure. He consented to have them in the house, she can mention that."

A motion *in limine* (rhymes with Jiminy, as in "Cricket") is usually a motion in advance of trial. By moving *in limine*, counsel attempts to prevent the other side from bringing out information or evidence before a judge rules on something that is pending. Not to do so could affect the outcome of the trial, even cause a mistrial. In this case, a motion to suppress (the incriminating details of the halted search) submitted by the defense had yet to be ruled on; they had started the trial not knowing whether the jury would be permitted to hear this part of the story.

"Furthermore," went Conroy, "it is our belief that the State is trying to produce evidence of a homicide, charges which the State has already dropped. If they want to produce evidence toward the concealment, they are entitled to do so, but ... it is our position that she can't try to prove the homicide. She can prove a homicide happened, but she is not allowed to try to prove that the defendant committed the homicide."

In fact, the revised jury instructions said that the State must prove the following propositions: The defendant performed acts which concealed the death of Lynne Matchem-Thomas by hiding her body, and that when the defendant did so he knew that she had died by homicidal means. In this context, "concealed" requires something more than simply withholding knowledge or failing to disclose information. It involves "the performing of some act or acts for the purpose of preventing or delaying the discovery of a homicidal death."

So, in effect, the State had the burden of showing that a murder had occured and that the defendant knew the murder had occured. But it could not present evidence that Curtis Thomas committed that murder. Yet, the evidence the State would produce to prove the concealment charge would be so intertwined with the homicide-related evidence that, theoretically, to bar one set of evidence would be to bar the other.

It might have been a certified conundrum; Dobrinic as maestro conducting a symphony with her hands tied. In the end, however, Judge Huber denied Conroy's motion to suppress. The jury would hear of the halted search as well as other testimony highly damaging to the defendant. Curtis' activities and behaviors as relating to the charges were to be published for the enlightenment of the jury, and the jurors, in turn, were to consider only that evidence which spoke to *concealment* of a homicide and were not to infer that the defendant committed said homicide or was ever charged with murder.

Dobrinic continued, outlining her case against

Curtis. It sounded solid. She cited a veritable mountain of evidence, all of it circumstantial *except* for the upcoming direct testimony of the State's key witness, Deborah Claybrook, who would tell, in chilling detail, of Curtis' forthright confession to her and only to her.

"She will tell you, ladies and gentlemen, how the defendant said to her, as they listened to a radio talk show on the subject of battered women, how he had said, 'I have committed the ultimate battery.'"

Kathryn Dobrinic was pacing, appealing to the jury, who had promised to show common sense. "There is a saying, ladies and gentlemen, I don't know if you have heard it: God is in the details. This case is a detailed case and there's a lot to keep track of. There is plenty of evidence that proves this defendant guilty. It's evidence that corroborates one another. Things that Deborah Claybrook will tell you are corroborated by police officers and search warrants. By the end of the trial you will see how all this fits together, these pieces, what they mean, the picture they make. And when you see this, ladies and gentlemen, there's no reasonable conclusion you can reach except that the defendant is guilty of concealment of a homicide in our county."

Actually, she had it wrong. "The devil is in the details" is the common variety of that phrase. Dobrinic had her metaphors mixed up, but that was one of her few missteps. She had done her homework on the case, had the jurors captivated by her down-home sensible style, and she was bound and determined to put Curtis away for a good long time.

TWENTY-ONE

Right off, in his opening statement, Conroy attempted to impugn Deborah Claybrook.

"... she will testify that Curtis made statements to her. She will testify that she has testified previously before a grand jury, under oath, that she slept with this man after he told her he was a murderer. She didn't give any details how this supposed murder happened. No physical evidence was ever found through testimony she gave. More importantly, she told the grand jury that he poured gasoline all over the body and lit it. The State's own forensic people will testify there were no accelerants, that no gasoline was used. The State will never be able to explain how the only details that this woman gave of this crime were wrong.

"... what she will admit, if she is truthful, is that this man broke off his relationship with her, that this man had always suspected that the body over here could have been the body of his ex-wife.

"You'll also hear testimony how Curtis' house was

searched by an FBI team from Quantico, Virginia, and they spent days combing every inch of that basement and that house with high-tech equipment looking for the smallest bit of evidence — a drop of blood, a hair, anything to substantiate that this man did what he is accused of. They spent thousands of dollars and found nothing, and that's the best evidence this man has."

Here Conroy inadvertently belittled his client's upcoming testimony. Curtis' account, his word, *is* evidence, though admittedly not the sort of physical evidence Conroy was referring to.

Conroy went on to say the State's whole case was built on suspicion and mere circumstance, not hard facts. As soon as Lynne's body was identified, Conroy suggested, Curtis became a suspect primarily because of convenience to the police: He was the husband with a checkered past and he was around town, available, as it were, for the collaring.

"This has been a rush to judgment from the beginning," Conroy told the jury, who had promised not to "decide that somebody in this courtroom has got to pay."

He then turned to the thorny issue of the victim's "severe psychological problems." Lynne was under a psychiatrist's care precisely because she was unstable. She had wandered off before; she had been in a bar fight. She was unpredictable, "yet this man tried to stay with her. Finally, he threw up his hands and she disappeared."

He emphasized the discrepancies in the eyewitness accounts: "You will hear testimony from people who were out at the lake, that the van they saw was a van with no windows. It was a UPS-like cargo van, yet the van in the pictures presented by the State does not fit the descriptions. There's no license plate to tie this van to the defendant. There is no person that can identify this man. There is no witness who can testify that this man had anything to do with anything. What you have is the testimony of the bereaved mother, of a jilted lover and policemen who prejudged the case. All we ask you to do is keep an open mind, listen to all the evidence and be fair."

TWENTY-TWO

For the State, Dobrinic called three young men to the stand. Each in their turn would describe the red-orange van and its actions in the campground the night of May 8, 1993.

Nathan Gerl of Litchfield said he and his wife were at the lake around 10:15 and saw the fire at the edge of the woods. They never got out of the car. In fact, they "didn't want to be around because there weren't supposed to be fires there." They left the area and drove to Circle Marina — the Point — and, four or five minutes later, coming up the hill toward them was "a red van, a Ford Econoline."

How do you know it was a Ford Econoline? queried Dobrinic.

"I've worked on Fords," said Gerl, a mechanic with a heavy-equipment company. "I knew it by the body."

She brought out the enlarged, mounted photo of the Independence Center van. Yes, said Nathan Gerl, the van in the photo resembled the van he saw that night. No, he didn't get a look at the driver.

Josh Hogsett, 18, of Litchfield, was riding around with two buddies in a Grand Prix. Sometime between 10:15 and 10:30 they saw a fire and a red van parked next to the fire. It was a large fire. It "looked like bales burning."

Hogsett said he saw someone getting into the van. A silhouette. During the initial investigation, he told police it was a male.

Conroy seized on this during cross-exam: "How could you tell whether the subject was a male or female?"

"I can't describe it," replied Hogsett. "It was a man."

"OK, what made you think it was a man?"

"I don't know," said Hogsett, "didn't seem right a woman would be doing it."

Conroy later scored another point, asking, "Is it fair to say if you saw a 'colored man' out there you would've told the investigating officer you saw a colored man?"

Hogsett responded in the affirmative.

It is odd, yet revealing that the liberal-minded Conroy would use the term "colored." Not black or African-American. It's not likely that he would have used the antiquated sobriquet in front of a St. Louis jury. He may have thought this was the term with which Hogsett would identify.

Hogsett and his pals also headed down to the Point, a social hub of the recreation area. They stayed for awhile and then continued back along the main road. That's when they saw the van again. It pulled off a dirt road and then cut out in front of them on the paved park road, going fast. There was a blue pickup between

At one point the van was right, I mean *right* behind us

them and the van, and its headlights shone directly on the back doors of the van. As the van accelerated, Hogsett said, the right rear door suddenly swung open and they saw what looked like black plastic trash bags flapping in the rear of the cargo area.

Hogsett testified he saw the van again. On the way home after midnight it crossed his path on Union Avenue, in Litchfield, heading into the Huck's parking lot. It was 12:30, two hours after the initial sighting.

As he stepped down from the witness stand, Hogsett told Dobrinic, "Good luck." Curtis hunched toward his attorney, whispering, and Conroy was at the bench in a flash. "My client wants to recall the witness, your honor. He says it goes to bias."

"Well, it's your case," replied Judge Huber, "and you can put him on for that purpose if you heard the statement and that's what happened."

Conroy huffed a bit, and said he wanted it noted for the record.

John Reeves' testimony was even more intriguing. The van chased him and his date!

At 10 p.m. Reeves closed his family's video store. He and his girlfriend had planned to go to the drive-in, but they went to the lake instead. In their Mercury Topaz they first saw the van sitting back on the gravel road of Picnic Area 5, close to the main road. John Reeves, who had been "in and out of automotive," said he knew the vehicle to be a Ford van from its headlights and taillights, which were lighted as they approached, but went out as they passed. Reeves and his girlfriend laughed at this. "Must be kids partying in there," they said.

They drove on, ending up, like the others, at the Point. A short time later, still in the park and heading east on Arrowhead Road — Rollercoaster Road, as the townies call it — they saw the red van coming down a hill ahead of them. They passed, going in opposite directions, but soon after, to Reeves' amazement, the van was tailing them. The driver had spun a U-ey.

"It was racing up behind," Reeves told Dobrinic. "You could hear it kicking in the passing gear, catching up. It would lose us on the curves and catch up on the straightaways. At one point the van was right, I mean *right* behind us," he said dramatically.

Reeves turned down a side road and the van followed. There were no other cars around, just them, and
with the van's headlights piercing the dark inside of
their car they were really starting to get scared. There
was another crossroad coming up, Reeves knew, and he
decided this would be the place to try to ditch their
pursuer. He pressed the accelerator, got the Topaz up to
60, and just as the road came up he braked slightly and
whipped it to the the right, spewing dust and gravel.

They stopped about 15 yards into the turn and waited. The van had missed the turn, but it, too, stopped
just past the intersection. The two vehicles were now
perpendicular to one another. John Reeves and his girlfriend stayed in their car, waiting to see what would
happen. The van just rested there ominously in the
middle of the road; they could hear its rough idle.
Finally, after some tense moments, the van turned
around, heading back the way it had come.

The next day when John Reeves read about the
body, he wondered if there might be a connection
between the murder and the menacing van. He told his
parents what had happened and they told him to go to
the police. All right, he said, but first he wanted to
retrace his movements of the previous evening. He
used the same car, went by the same clock and took
exactly the same route. The only thing different was
the time of day. By his reckoning, he first saw the van
parked at No. 5 at 10:12 p.m. The last time he saw it
was 10:50.

John Reeves called the police and volunteered
everything he knew. His statement totaled seven pages
and was specific to the point of naming the song on the
radio when the van was first spotted.

He described the vehicle as "a Ford three-quarter ton, bright-orange cargo van with heavy duty wheels. No windows on back or sides. I saw Missouri plates, which I felt were black with yellow or gold lettering."

Now, at that time, the only plates issued by the Missouri Department of Revenue that have gold lettering on a black background were the so-called vanity plates, the ones which people pay extra for and often have cute little words or phrases such as EIEIO, HUMBUG or H8TOW8. However, the commercial plates issued by the Missouri Department of Motor Vehicles had white lettering on either a blue background or a black background. The plates on the cargo van from Independence Center, the one that Curtis was supposed to have used that night, had white letters and numerals on a black background.

John Reeves studied the enlarged photo known as People's Exhibit No. 7. "It is a Ford van," he said. "A panel van, very similar to the one I saw." Then he threw in a qualifier. "But it's not as heavy duty a van as what I saw. It's lighter. The one I saw was more a cargo-type van."

Also problematic were the windows on the rear doors of the van pictured in People's Exhibit No. 7. Reeves had said there were no windows. Dobrinic got Reeves to qualify that the van had no windows *from his point of view*, that is, seeing most of the van but not all of it. As if to say there actually was a window, but it was in his blind spot.

Conroy, on recross, said to Reeves, "And if you had seen windows you would have wrote that down on your statement like you wrote down the details of the song on the radio that you heard, correct?"

"Correct," echoed Reeves.

On this same issue Pat Conroy would later grab at straws with some of the witnesses he brought in, such as Nance Jarman of Litchfield. Her testimony took only a few minutes, but Conroy was hoping that the mere suggestion of a white guy in the scenario might plant doubt in the jurors' minds. After establishing that Jarman was at a Litchfield gas station around 11 a.m. on May 8, 1993, he asked her to please describe what she saw.

"I seen a Caucasian man driving a van," she answered.

"What kind of a van?"

"Rust-colored, kind of orange, and that's all I know."

Brilliant. And, of course, Curtis would have been at work at 11 a.m. that day. Besides, it went to show that vans, orange or red or even orange-reddish colored, would not be uncommon in Litchfield, especially along the gas-up, fast-food strip next to the interstate.

TWENTY-THREE

"This is a view of the body at the time of the autopsy, on the autopsy table. Here, as you can see, the legs are severely charred, as a result of fire, and portions of the lower extremities are actually skeletonized in that the tissues have fallen away from the bone ..."

Curtis had received Judge Huber's permission to leave the courtroom during the autopsy slide show. He didn't want to see the remains of his wife even more sliced and diced than he had already imagined. The jurors had already been cautioned about the grisly nature of the pictures.

Dr. Travis Hindman, a distinguished-looking physician in his late-50s, provided the narration. He had been pathologist of record at Springfield Memorial Medical Center when Janie Doe's body arrived at 4:30 a.m. on May 9, 1993. He had started the autopsy at 8 a.m. with the help of two histotechnologists, two radiology technicians and a medical photographer. Special Agent Mike Sheeley and Crime Scene Technician Paul Schuh, up all night with the case, were there as well.

Janie Doe was one of more than a thousand autopsies that Hindman had performed in his long career. Like Mark Johnsey, he, too, ventured the observation that she was Caucasian. Pointer in hand, the doctor continued with his narration.

" ... the hands are bagged in paper, which is considered to be the standard in terms of preservation of evidence on the hands. This is a view of the right side of the body from a slightly forward angle. This is the left shoulder, this is the right shoulder. You can see the absence of a head. This is the base of the neck, which is charred ..."

The jury sat stock still, mesmerized by the obscenity of mutilation depicted on the screen. There was not so much as a nervous clearing of the throat.

" ... this is the breast tissue here, which is charred. This region right in here is the location where the skin has been partially peeled away by heat and the skin underneath is lighter than the skin here that's on the surface. In addition to that, you are able then to see the streaks of what appears to me to be blood ...

"This shows the posterior view of the severely charred buttocks, the low back region" — the pointer darted from locus to locus — "the legs split with the absence of an enormous amount of skin."

"Are these exhibits," inquired Kathryn Dobrinic, "fair and accurate depictions of the way the body appeared to you the day you performed the autopsy in 1993?"

Hindman said they were.

"Now, doctor, you indicated that one of your purposes in doing such an examination is to try to determine a cause of death, is that correct?"

Hindman said it was.

"Was there anything you observed about this body that would help you determine the cause of death?"

"Only in very general terms."

"What is that, sir?"

"The head of the decedent was absent, and in inspection of the remainder of the body I was not able to find any evidence of a wound or wounds which might have caused the death. In addition, there were no toxicologic findings that in any way would have significantly contributed to or caused death. I could not find any disease processes which would have contributed to or caused death. The injuries, insofar as we could identify at autopsy, were those of a thermal nature and the absence of a head."

On the face of it, it seems obvious that a headless woman would have died of decapitation, but as any student of Holmes — Sherlock, not Oliver Wendell — knows, the truth may be masked by astounding circumstance. Conveniently, the mortality rate among schizophrenics has been extensively studied, and it is well known that that population suffers from a high incidence of suicides and fatal accidents. One researcher, Eugen Bleuler, noted that the suicidal drive is the most serious of all schizophrenic symptoms. In 1973, Osmond and Hoffer, in a review of six reports, concluded that the suicide rate among the schizophrenic population is 20 times higher than that among the general population. Though Matchem-Thomas was not formally diagnosed as schizophrenic, she did have a psychotic disorder for which she was being treated with Haldol, the same anti-psychotic drug widely used for treatment of schizophrenia.

Given that, there are numerous scenarios in which the decedent might have taken her own life. Was it possible, for instance, that Lynne hanged herself with piano wire and, leaping from a height, her head snapped off? Curtis or someone else took her to the sticks to avoid publicity and save funeral expenses. Unlikely, but stranger things have happened.

Back to Dr. Hindman. Did he at least have any *opinion* on the cause of death?

"No, as I indicated on the report to the coroner, the cause of death was undetermined, and I feel, from the standpoint of the autopsy, no different now from what I felt at the time."

"And what is standing in the way of you determining the cause of death of this individual?" inquired the prosecutor.

"There are a multiplicity of things," replied Hindman, "that can happen to an individual's head to cause death. That would include drowning, smothering, bludgeoning, gunshot wounds. There's a long list of things that could have happened."

OK, he couldn't arrive at the cause of death. Then what about a time of death?

"The standard method of determining time of death is based on post-mortem rigidity — rigor mortis — the stiffness of the extremities," the pathologist patiently explained. "But this could not be used as a means of evaluation, because of thermal injury, the virtual cooking of the tissues.

"Another method is that of post-mortem lividity,"

continued Hindman. "Whenever an individual dies and is lying in one position, the blood descends to the lowest portions of the body and the skin can appear discolored on those areas. If this discoloration, due to the settling of blood, becomes fixed in the tissues, it can give us certain parameters which can be used to determine an approximate time of death. Though, because of the severe thermal injury and distortion of the skin by heat, this, too, was of no help."

There was yet another way of determining a time of death, said Hindman, the post-mortem vitreous-humor potassium evaluation. The vitreous humor is a fluid contained in the eyeball. In the hours and days after death, there is a predictable change in several features of the vitreous humor. The most commonly and most reliably tested feature is the potassium level in the vitreous humor. Obviously, the means to perform that test were not available.

Depending on the environment in which it rests, a body decomposes at a relatively set rate. With Janie Doe, however, the fire had essentially stopped the putrefaction of the body. The flames had fixed her decomposition, stressed Dr. Hindman, "almost like a photograph" of the time in which the body was roasted.

Dr. Hindman testified that no sperm was found in her body cavities, and that no drugs of any detectable level were identified in her blood, though he did report that at the time of autopsy Janie Doe had a blood alcohol level of .075 percent. At the time, .010 percent was considered to be legally intoxicated, and the state of Illinois has since succeeded in lowering that limit to .08 percent.

Conroy, in his cross-examination, seized on the presence of alcohol in Janie Doe's system and, after a long-winded digression by Hindman, he got him to simply agree that the measurable percentages of blood alcohol can decrease after death, though not significantly. The liver may continue to metabolize drugs and alcohol even after cardiac death. Too, the post-mortem action of bacteria, yeast, fungus and other microbes may alter the level of blood alcohol.

Certainly, Conroy wanted to emphasize for the jurors that Lynne was drinking up to the time of her death, perhaps in a bar, perhaps with her killer. Where had she been between Wednesday afternoon and Saturday evening: in a cardboard coffin in Curtis' basement or out carousing? You could see the little wheels turning in Pat Conroy's head.

TWENTY-FOUR

Another set of jurors were trying the case in a separate court of law, specifically the dining room of the Red Rooster Inn, just off the town square. The $3.49 salad bar made a good lunch, but stay away from the macaroni salad. There was Pete Bastian, the St. Louis attorney in private practice who had come up with me for the day. Pete, who in the mid '70s, fresh out of law school, cut his legal teeth doing civil-rights work for indigent blacks in Southern Illinois, is about four shades more liberal than most attorneys. There was Ron Leible, the reporter for *The Montgomery County News*. Ron had graduated from the University of Missouri – Mizzou – with a degree in journalism, and it seemed he wrote half the stories in the *News*. He would eventually leave Hillsboro to work in St. Louis driving a delivery truck. And there was myself, a former venereal disease epidemiologist with the Center For Disease Control turned writer for a weekly tabloid.

As soon as we were seated and began chowing down, Bastian started in. "What bothers me most is they haven't proven the homicide."

"That's right!" I interjected. "He couldn't say how she died. Dr. Hindman couldn't say whether Lynne's death was the result of a homicide, a suicide or simply accidental."

Leible wagged his head in amazement. "How can someone can be criminally charged with concealing a murder victim when there's no empirical proof that a murder actually occurred?"

"Apparently, the grand jury bought into it," replied Bastian. "The way I see it, there's evidence to *support* a homicide because we have a dead body and a woman to say Curtis killed her, but the homicide is assumed."

"Strictly speaking," I offered, "all the State has is the allegation of Curtis moving a dead body."

" ... a nonviolent offense, a misdemeanor."

" ... or in some places, an ordinance violation.

"The Supreme Court has made it clear," said Bastian, "that the constitutional notion of a fair trial requires that *all* elements of a crime be proven beyond a reasonable doubt. I say that if the state can't prove that a murder was committed, then this case could and should be overturned and the defendant discharged."

"Wouldn't that be a kick?" said Leible.

"Why is he being tried here anyway?" Bastian went on. "If a guy from St. Louis dumps a body off a bridge in East St. Louis they don't try him in Illinois."

"Politics," said Ron. "Maybe the prosecutors struck a deal. Dobrinic's coming up for re-election. She needs a big feather in her warbonnet. Curtis and Conroy have been putting out the word that Curtis' conviction is that feather. They say that Dee Hayes in St. Louis did Dobrinic a favor by giving up Curtis, and she'll collect

126

on it when the time is right. That's just a theory."
Leible had to be careful in his pronouncements; his
boss at the newspaper, Richard Slepicka, editor, was
Kathryn Dobrinic's brother.

It was perplexing all right. We shoveled ham and
mashed potatoes into faces for a while, anticipating the
next round of discussion. The mysterious van, naturally.

On the face of it, we agreed, these eyewitness
accounts of the van in the campground seemed to belie
the actions of a person who was there that night to
dump a body, because whoever was in that van was in
no hurry to leave the scene of the crime — or not worried about being caught.

And why would a murderer make himself conspicu-
ous by tailing and harassing potential witnesses, afford-
ing them a better view of the vehicle and license plate?

And Circle Marina, where the van was seen by
Nathan Gerl and his girlfriend *after* the fire was set, is
away from the road that leads back to Interstate 70 and
St. Louis. From Picnic Area No. 5, the killer had only
to drive a short distance to be out of the campground,
home free as it were. Yet, he went further into it.

"There's definitely a puzzle in that," said Leible.
"What jumps in my mind is that maybe the killer was
trying to leave the scene but got turned around and
briefly lost."

We enjoyed these idle speculations. They were the
best part of trial watching. I put in my two cents worth.
"Maybe he was a really brazen criminal who enjoyed
toying with witnesses. On top of that he was stoned
and drunk out of his mind and didn't care what happened — whether he ran someone off the road, crashed
the van or got caught."

"Or, maybe," put in Bastian, blowing on a piping spoonful of soup, "he wasn't the body-dumper at all, so he wasn't worried about being seen. But even more baffling, if Josh Hogsett's last sighting was accurate, why was this clown still lingering near the crime scene two hours later when ..."

" ... he would have known the cops would be looking for a red-orange cargo van!" Leible interjected.

"That's risky business for a black man who would have been easily recalled, if spotted," I noted.

"Let's see," said Bastian, counting off his fingers. "We've got Reeves and his girl, Nathan Gerl and his wife, Hogsett and his two buddies. Did Burdell and Jett claim to see the van?"

"No," said Ron Leible, the most familiar with the case.

"OK," said Bastian. "By this count seven people saw the van at different places and different times and not one — not *one* — got a look at the driver or took down the license number."

"That's pretty damn strange," said Ron Leible.

"Yeah," I answered, "but people just aren't naturally observant that way. Can you name the types of beans in your three-bean salad? And don't look."

"Well, I know there's kidney beans," he began, "and some kind of yellow bean, a wax bean maybe and ... I really don't know," he chuckled, "just so long as it's tasty and nice to look at and doesn't bind me up."

"In the immortal words of Perry Mason, I rest my case," I said.

TWENTY-FIVE

Lynne did not come home the night of April 14. The following day she told Curtis she was moving in with her mother. She went to get some boxes to move her stuff. Did she go to Ryder or Budget truck rental to get boxes? No. Did she go to United Van Lines, Allied Van Lines or Atlas Van Lines? No. Did she go to Mayflower, Bekins or any of the several dozen local moving and storage companies to get her packing boxes? No, she went to U-Haul. And did she buy the more expensive double-ply box, less likely to break apart? No, she opted for the cheaper single-ply.

Off to the side of the bench there sat a couple of U-Haul boxes and some black trash bags. These things, the People's Exhibits, looked like clutter in the court-room. They made Curtis uneasy.

Moving, if you do it yourself, can take a long time. At the time of her disappearance, Lynne was still pack-ing her things into boxes; some of those boxes were at the Waterman address and some were in her mother's basement. The ones on Waterman were disposed of sometime after Lynne was reported missing — Curtis said he gave them to charity. But mothers can be quite sentimental, and the boxes in Shirley Matchem's basement were undisturbed when Detective Sheeley came calling in the fall of 1994.

Sheeley questioned her about everything. The fact that Lynne had been moving rang one of those bells that sometimes ring in a detective's suspicious mind. How far along had she gotten? Who was helping her? What was she using for transport? Shirley said she wasn't sure what sort of boxes Lynne had used, but he was welcome to look. Shirley took him down the steps and showed him a corner full of boxes that Lynne had already packed and brought home. There were also some black plastic trash bags that Lynne had used to line the U-Haul boxes. She was particular and wanted to protect her clothing.

Those boxes and trash bags, duly seized as evidence, were a cornerstone in the State's case. Kathryn Dobrinic would show that they represented a direct link between Curtis' residence and the crime scene. With carefully constructed questions put to cooperative witnesses, she was able to paint a picture, as vivid as that of any artist, of a body being put in a trash bag and then placed into a packing box.

ISP Crime Scene Technician Paul Schuh would testify that specific markings on the unburned portions of the material found under the body enabled forensic technicians to positively identify this material as a single-ply cardboard U-Haul packing box, that the black plastic trash bags found in Shirley's home, originally from Curtis' home, were consistent with the material fused into the victim's flesh.

The boxes and bags that looked like trash sitting there made Curtis uneasy because they had the potential to be incriminating. If they were not quite the feathers around the muzzle of the accused chicken killing dog, then they were at least the dog turd on the new carpet when there is but one dog in the house.

TWENTY-SIX

Pat Conroy pivoted, turning to Det. Mike Sheeley on the witness stand. Sheeley was in the midst of testifying about how police had combed Curtis' home looking for the alleged bucket of hardened concrete concealing a severed head. Conroy fixed the detective with a gloating look and asked whether the search had proven fruitful. Sheeley met Conroy's gaze and freely admitted it had not.

"Then where's the bucket?" demanded Conroy, jabbing a digit at the witness. "Where's the head?"

"I'd like to know," said Sheeley, plainly exasperated. "I don't."

They never did find the head. In fact, after Deborah Claybrook had told the cops about Curtis supposedly hiding the head in a bucket of concrete, Mike Sheeley contacted the FBI's Evidence Response Team in St. Louis.

In late August 1995, while Curtis was in jail, the evidence response team with engineering back-up from the bureau's Special Search Techniques Unit based in Quantico — the very ones who under noted forensic chemist Steven Burmeister had combed the blasted-out Murrah Federal Building in Oklahoma City a few months earlier — were methodically searching the Waterman address with an array of high-tech tools.

The fiber-optic scope, infra-red camera and ground-penetrating radar are commercially used for checking cracks in bridges and detecting leaks in pipelines. Only in the last 10 to 20 years have they been applied forensically as geophysical prospecting techniques for revealing potential evidence repositories — backyard graves or concealed spaces in buildings.

Prior to his arrest, Curtis had done some cement work on the porch and in the basement. It seemed odd and maybe too coincidental to have so much construction. These remodeled areas were highly focused on.

The agents ran ground-penetrating radar all over the basement floor. The detection of any anomalies called for the drilling of an inch-diameter hole in the concrete and the insertion of a micro-video camera on a flexible fiber-optic stem to search the hollow space within. "It's very effective," said a St. Louis based FBI agent who participated in the search and who requested anonymity, "and the big up-side is you don't have to tear out the entire basement floor to find out what's under it. With this technology you can pinpoint where you want to look."

The fresh patches of concrete down in the basement intrigued the agents, but all they concealed was plumbing.

Then where's the bucket? Where's the head?

They checked for voids in the walls, went through his cupboards and closets. They dismantled the plumbing to check the traps and drains. Until now, physical evidence in the case had been as scarce as liquor at a tent revival. If there was one iota of physical evidence, anything from a hair to dried droplet of blood to a head in a bucket, it was going to be found.

They checked the yard too, with both a magnetometer — a metal detector — and by means of infra-red thermography. As the FBI agent explained, "All day the sun beats down on the ground. At night that energy is reflected back into the atmosphere. If you have a grave or a hole dug, the energy will be reflected differently from the relative coolness of the grave than from the undisturbed ground around it. The infra-red camera picks up that difference. Now, in the backyard we did find a grave and that happened to be the remains of a cat."

In the end, they came up empty-handed. Well, not quite true. They did confiscate a couple of bags of cement mix, some spackling compound, some paint thinner and a two-and-a-half-gallon gasoline can from the rear of the house. But what did that prove? That he uses the same hardware store supplies as every other homeowner who does his own yard and housework.

The agent said he wasn't particularly surprised at the absence of a tangible find. "In a situation like that where you have dumpsters around, there are more convenient ways to get rid of something rather than to bury it or wall it up, but you've got to rule out everything."

The Independence Center van had long been sold and was still in use by a heating-and-cooling outfit. It, too, was subjected to thorough forensic analysis. Results: nothing.

After two days, the elite FBI forensics team gave up their search.

Because Claybrook testified that Curtis admitted hiding the head, the fact that the head could not be produced served to bolster the defense's assertion that Claybrook was making things up.

TWENTY-SEVEN

The accelerants issue was a bit more dicey. Deborah Claybrook asserted that Curtis had mentioned that he had poured gasoline over the body "to keep the wild animals away." This was a bizarre and puzzling statement coming from Curtis via his "medium," Claybrook, because if he meant to torch the body forthwith there would be no need to keep the wild things at bay — the body would not be unattended, as it were. And what sort of wild animals might find their way in to Curtis' basement? A rat, a squirrel, a wily urban possum perhaps, but nothing to bother a corpse in holdover for a few days. The wild animal comment never was clarified. At any rate, Claybrook had Curtis saying that when he to light the body on that May evening in Litchfield, the sudden bright flash — magnified by the gasoline — had startled him. Yet, ISP Crime Scene Technician Paul Schuh had already testified that he had tested for and found no presence of accelerants at the scene. That was a feather in the cap of the defense. The prosecution, however, would pluck that feather.

Dobrinic brought in Eric Young, a forensic scientist with the State Police Crime Lab in Springfield. Young specializes in the field of trace chemistry. He analyzes the minute and residual evidence found, for example, in arson or bombing cases. He was stipulated as an expert witness.

Young studied People's Exhibits Numbers 21, 22 and 23. Yes, he recognized them. They are containers on which he had done arson analysis. Dobrinic asked him to explain.

"Essentially, we test debris from fires to determine the presence or absence of, say, flammable liquids. Things like kerosene, gasoline, lighter fluid."

"Would you please elaborate?"

"The evidence is usually submitted in a sealed container," Young began. "We punch two holes in the top of this container, insert some tubes that contain charcoal, a very absorbent substance much like sawdust. We then place the container into an oven, and we hook up one of the tubes to a vacuum pump. As the oven heats, any residue of petroleum products inside the container will rise to the top and be drawn out by the vacuum pump through the charcoal and actually be absorbed onto the charcoal. We then wash this tube with a solvent and do some instrumental tests — gas chromatography and mass spectrometry — to determine the presence of an accelerant."

Young replied to Dobrinic's question that the contents of these containers were represented to him to be soil and debris from the Janie Doe fire scene. Could he tell the ladies and gentlemen the results of the test?

"I found no flammable or combustible liquids to be present."

Ditto the findings for People's Exhibit Number 24, "a piece of skin from the victim of the fire."

So far, so good. "Now, in your expert opinion," she said, raising her voice a notch for the benefit of the hard-of-hearing, "does this mean that accelerants were never present on these items?"

"No, it doesn't mean that," replied Young. "Any time an accelerant is used there's always the possibility it could be totally consumed during the course of a fire. And there's also the possibility — well, what happens occasionally, the materials in the fire can give off byproducts which we refer to as pyrolysis product. And sometimes, on our instrumentation, these byproducts can mask small amounts of a potential accelerant."

Not only that, Young went on to say, but if the sample is improperly packaged, exposed to air even a little, the accelerant can evaporate. And if the accelerant was present but exposed to windy or humid conditions it would evaporate more rapidly. Exposure to moisture, too, may interfere with the analysis. There are a lot of reasons an accelerant wouldn't be detected, said Young, but those are the major ones.

You could see the jury mulling this over. There was no gasoline, but there *might* have been. There was no head in a bucket of concrete, but there *might* have been. Deborah Claybrook was not lying under oath about these details, but she *might've* been.

TWENTY-EIGHT

Kathryn Dobrinic said it was the most complicated case she had ever tried. Logistically, it was difficult scheduling the appearances of 30 some witnesses from St. Louis, some of whom had to be taxied by squad car.

One witness who came in his own police car was Jim Bell, a case coordinator with the Palatine (Illinois) Police Department. Before that, for four years, Bell was a major-case specialist for the FBI, in Quantico. With a resume of investigative credits running eight pages, Bell is a homicide enthusiast. He has consulted to or been involved in the investigation of nearly every high-profile mass murder or serial murders of the last 20 years, including the Hillside Strangler case, the Green River murders and the Ted Bundy murders, as well as the massacre at Brown's Chicken restaurant in his own bailiwick of Palatine.

Stipulated as an expert witness for the prosecution, he testified that if body parts are mutilated or removed it is often a deliberate attempt to slow down the ensuing investigation. With only a human torso, investigators have no solid starting point.

Said Bell: "Routinely, once an identification of a homicide victim is made, the investigators know what circles this person moved in. Now, if someone close to that victim believes they will be the suspect they may go to great lengths to conceal the identity. Otherwise they're brought into the investigation right away, and they have to have answers."

And the killer of Lynne Matchem-Thomas had a long time to get his story straight.

Bell also said that a clever killer might move a body from one city to another or even one state to another, causing problems for police because different jurisdictions don't communicate well — not necessarily because they're uncooperative or fiercely territorial, but because they're not set up that way. That same clever killer, Bell added, might also undress the victim.

"Usually," said Bell, "when we find the victims have been stripped down and all of their clothing removed as well as personal effects — jewelry, purse, wallet, shoes, whatever — again, it's a deliberate attempt to destroy evidence. The killer is taking hairs and fibers and other minute bits of evidence that may not even be visible but which could aid in the identification. So they strip the homicide victim to make sure the police don't have the ability to even get to that stage of the investigation."

Conroy, during cross-exam, got Bell to agree that the removal of a victim's feet and hands would also delay the identification. If this clever killer were to go to the trouble of removing the head why not do the job right and take the extremities as well, subtract every last means of identification.

But as it happened, Conroy had a hidden agenda with Bell. He wanted to question him about the search of Curtis' house by the FBI, get him to say how thorough they were and how if there had been anything related to Lynne's murder they would have found it. As he started, Dobrinic objected that this was beyond the scope of direct examination. Conroy reminded her that Bell was qualified as an expert in the field of homicide investigation.

They needed a referee. At the sidebar, Judge Huber told Conroy his line of questioning was beyond the scope, but that he could recall Bell if he would subpoena him.

They had just left the bench conference when Dobrinic returned, asking to state something for the record. "He just made a snide comment to me in front of the jury. I don't appreciate it," she told Huber.

Conroy began to protest, but she cut him off. "I don't think he should make speeches," she said.

"There should not be speeches in front of the jury," agreed the judge.

"That goes for both parties," urged Conroy. "I ask the court to instruct ..."

Dobrinic cut him off again, her eyes flashing. "I object and renew my objection to defense counsel's speeches."

Conroy was there to represent Curtis. Dobrinic, presumably, to see that justice was done. They could use every legal trick in the book to press their case. They could cajole, flatter or browbeat witnesses, they could object until they were blue in the face, but ultimately the attorneys were supposed to be professional and businesslike. Nothing personal. Throughout this trial, however, the prosecutor and defense attorney sparred so often they could have starred in their own sit-com, The Battling Barristers. Their relationship was not quite as hostile as owls and crows, who will harass each other on sight, but the rancor was certainly transparent. With her pursed lips and arched brow, Dobrinic seemed to be holding in some strong emotion and, indeed, both seemed agitated or even outraged by the actions of the other.

At one point, Conroy was questioning a witness and speaking to the jury when she broke in. "Objection, your honor. He's lecturing the jury. He's been doing this all week." Conroy counterpunched with the objection that Dobrinic was "showboating," which, if you've ever seen the Delta Queen plying the Mississippi on a starlit night, could be considered a compliment.

As for James Bell, Mr. Homicide, Conroy never did subpoena him. When prosecution and defense were finished with him he took his leave and presumably rushed off to the next breaking mass murder.

TWENTY-NINE

On a balmy Palm Sunday in 1991, Pat Conroy and Martha Sandner decided to exercise their constitutional right to free speech by publicly burning an American flag. Contrarily, some other First Amendment practitioners in the vicinity decided to exercise their muscles by beating the crap out of the flag burners.

Conroy, an assistant public defender in St. Louis, had met Sandner the year before while taking a bar-exam prep course at St. Louis University. Of like mind — young, Catholic and politically active — they fell in love. They became engaged. Then came Desert Storm, a conflict they adamantly opposed on political and religious grounds. As activists, they had to act.

For months, The Old Post Office on Market Street in downtown St. Louis had been the site of a muscle-flexing patriotic demonstration. Every Sunday the group would assemble to sing, wave flags and shout at passing cars. Support the troops, they yelled. Bomb Iraq. Respect the flag.

Conroy and Sandner stood across the street from the rowdy assembly. They picked the highly visible spot because, Sandner would tell a reporter, "If you're discreet, you don't get your message across."

Sandner clutched her Bible. She intended to say a prayer for peace over the flames. As they readied to torch the lighter fluid-soaked flag they had brought, as many as 15 rabid demonstrators ran across Market Street and attacked them. They threw the couple to the ground. They kicked them and spat in their faces. They called them traitors and told them to go back to Iraq. By the time police arrived Sandner had a broken wrist. The flag was unscorched.

Police charged Sandner, Conroy and two others with disturbing the peace. The arrests made the news, and the following day Conroy was flooded with angry phone calls at his work; some were death threats. Conroy was uncontrite. "It's time for the flag-wavers of this war to clean up their filthy mess," he wrote in a letter to the editor of a local newspaper. "American flags will be burned until they do."

Imagining Kathryn Dobrinic burning a flag in protest or even uttering something remotely seditious is like trying to imagine snow in Hawaii.

If there was ever a greater contrast in the styles of two attorneys, it would be hard to find. About the only thing they had in common was a stake in the outcome of Curtis Thomas' fate. And possibly that neither was a Republican.

Kathryn Dobrinic was slight of frame with piercing blue eyes, a long sloping bridge and parted-in-the-middle wavy blond hair, naturally unruly or possibly the result of a permanent gone awry. She had the hard-

She intended to say a prayer for peace over the flames

around-the-edges look of one of those depression-era sharecropper women in a Dorothea Lange photograph. Still, you could imagine her in jeans and T-shirt, sipping beer, standing around the barbeque pit at the annual bar association picnic. In the courtroom, however, she was the very model of propriety, looking every inch the State's attorney in her light-gray business suit and white blouse buttoned to the top. She was quick and assertive, too, at times pouncing on some testimony or point of procedure like a jungle cat. Having seen me speaking to Curtis during a jury break, for instance, she was quick to confront.

You were talking to the defendant?

You saw me.

What did he have to say to you?

Just that he feels he should have a change of venue.

Dobrinic sized me up with a critical gaze. Don't

leave, she said authoritatively, you're a witness. Of course, I was never called. It was simply a nudge of intimidation, her way of letting me know my place: You're here in a passive capacity, to observe and report. Not to participate.

If Dobrinic was a wound-up mainspring, Conroy was an unraveled ball of yarn. His personal appearance was, to put it kindly, casual for the courtroom. His checkered sport jacket spent a good deal of time draped on the back of his chair. His shirt sleeves were rolled, his tie loosened. He would almost recline in his seat, elbow crooked on the back of the chair, ankle propped up on the knee of the other leg. He was *lounging*. If the courtroom were a baseball stadium, Conroy would have been a salesman at an afternoon doubleheader.

Unlike Dobrinic, Conroy rarely addressed the court from the podium, but preferred the sitting position. When called to approach the bench and forced, as it were, to ambulate, he decidedly listed to one side like a ship taking on water. At first, I felt sorry for him — scoliosis is a pitiable condition — though ultimately I came to believe it was nothing more serious than bad posture.

Conroy had a quiet, methodical sense about him which could play well to a rural jury, if only he could have masked his irascibility. He also needed to project. The preponderance of his remarks were barely audible to those in the rear of the courtroom, except when he objected. Pat Conroy objected frequently and strenuously, and he was overruled most of the time.

PART III

THIRTY

"I think she was attracted to him because of his intellectual abilities," said Herman Jimerson. The attorney was in his office talking about his friend Lynne Matchem's first encounter with her future husband.

"They met at the library, you know. Curtis walked up and made his move. He gave her his address on Waterman, and he wrote it as the compound for water, H_2O, and the medical symbol for man. The circle with the arrow sticking out? And that's what caught her. She was intrigued by that. She showed it to me in philosophy class at Forest Park Community College. She thought it was the cleverest thing. I was more circumspect. I told her not to fall for it, but after I met him and saw them together I thought, 'These are two people who like each other.'"

Jimerson kept up with both Curtis and Lynne until she left St. Louis to work in San Diego for the U.S. Naval Warfare Station, in the computer room. "She was always interested in computers and saw computer technology as the key to her future," said Jimerson.

Curtis made several trips to San Diego and eventually succeeded in wooing her away. "He really wanted her," recalled the dapper attorney, gazing out on Clayton's Bonhomme Avenue. "He said she was the smartest woman he ever had."

On October 3, 1987, Curtis and Lynne were married in a private ceremony in Curtis' home on Waterman Avenue. They had known each other about 10 years. Curtis ran the Final Edition newsstand and Lynne attended college.

On their modest incomes, they enjoyed entertaining friends with small dinner parties at their home.

Herman Jimerson, by this time graduated from law school, was a frequent guest at these soirees. "They were such gracious hosts," he recalled. "Lynne was lovely, as ever, a little lonely perhaps. She liked good wine and they would always have a wonderful vintage at the table. Curtis would talk about some book he was reading or jump up and put on another album — he had a great jazz collection. I had many great times with the two of them. They were special to me and they never argued in my presence."

Yet, argue they did. As time passed they had become famous among their friends for their verbal fisticuffs.

"They came over to my house for dinner, and they growled at each other like two wet cats," said Curtis' cohort Rick Flynn, chuckling at the memory.

Lisa Randele, a postal worker and aspiring artist, was friendly with Lynne and, to a lesser degree, with Curtis. She recalled how "they used to argue a lot, very passionately, both of them. Each would try to convince me to be on their side, but I didn't want to get in the middle. I would joke with them and say, 'You both should study the law, the way you argue.'

"Lynne had a lot of opinions, which she felt strongly about," Randele continued, "and she would get so upset because Curtis would argue back in this calm, monotone voice, sometimes twisting her words around and sometimes insulting her in this icy manner. The more excited she got, the more impassive he got, and it would infuriate her."

Over time, Lynne grew depressed; she began self-medicating with beer and wine. She used marijuana. Meanwhile, Curtis was becoming more controlling. Michelle Matchem, Lynne's sister-in-law, interviewed by Det. Sheeley and Inspector Burwitz at her home in Evansville, Indiana, related that Lynne told her that Curtis made continuous demands on her for sex and he, being a vegetarian, tried to stop her from eating meat.

At times, their arguments went beyond mere name-calling. Michelle Matchem also described a slapping fight between Curtis and Lynne that occurred during a visit to Evansville in 1989. As the argument progressed, she told the agents, Curtis simply took off, leaving Lynne to find her own way back to St. Louis about 180 miles away.

By the early '90s, Curtis and Lynne's marriage was on the brink of ruin. Having to get a restraining order is never a good sign. Keep in mind that a restraining order is an *ex parte* action, a one-sided hearing. It simply means that one of the parties, the petitioner, has been able to get to a judge and that judge has issued an order based on that person's story. Never mind that the petitioner might be lying through his or her teeth, the judge, in 98 percent of the cases, will issue the order of protection simply because allegations of domestic violence must be taken seriously. The spouse or live-in will stand before a judge no later than 15 days after being served, and get to tell their side of the story. The judge may rescind the order or he may not. Having said that, a ranking officer in the St. Louis Sheriff's Department told me in confidence that "fifty percent of all restraining orders are bullshit," people using them to get even with spouses and lovers, to make them look bad.

In the text of that restraining order, granted to Lynne in October 1990, the part where the complainant tells what happened, she stated, "I was physically attacked by the respondent (Curtis). It was not a matter, as he might suggest, of him restraining me from destroying his property. I was thrown down continuously, kicked, punched, etc."

It was neither the first nor the last time the physical abuse would occur.

Money, or lack thereof, was another problem. "They were two promising people," said Herman Jimerson. "Curtis loved Lynne and Lynne loved Curtis very much. They seemed like a good match, but one thing led to another, and they couldn't get it going. They may have been over their heads with the house. Curtis had a couple of business failures and had gone to bankruptcy. Lynne was not making enough to make a difference. She was always in school, trying to get somewhere."

Ultimately, college was too taxing. Lynne ended up leaving her studies, though she would tell everyone it was only temporary.

In professional counseling there is a saying: No one is to blame, everyone is responsible. It is a good adage in that, ideally, it causes each party to reflect on how

As in Toronto, the victim was a cat

they might try to be a part of the solution; it is a belief
that, if practiced, stops resentment in its tracks. The
adage, however, doesn't neccesarily imply that the
involved parties are *equally* responsible for their problems at hand. In fact, the measure of culpability may be
and often is lopsided — 60/40, say, or even 80/20. In
short: Lynne may have egged him on, but Curtis had
himself a big slice of the Marital Discord Pie.

"He would mess her mind up," says Shirley
Matchem of Curtis. "Whenever she tried to study for a
test he would argue with her. He used to say she was
the smartest woman he'd ever known so why should he
want to aggravate her like that? It's hard to be orga-
nized when you've got so many problems in your

home."

Life with Curtis may have been enough to drive anyone over the edge. One way he toyed with Lynne, according to her mother, was by removing parts from her car so she couldn't get to school or work. It was as if he was punishing her for something she'd done. This ties in with statements Lynne made on the restraining order. She wrote, under heading No. 10, *I am afraid because*: "Prior to the physical attack, for at least a week, I was harassed. I believe he did and has in the past sabotaged my vehicle. He turned the water and the heat off, changed the phone number and put restraints on the line so I could not utilize it. Listens to my phone conversations and takes my belongings whenever he wishes."

But the pattern of abuse was not limited to his spouse. Again, Curtis displayed his penchant for animal cruelty. As in Toronto, the victim was a cat.

"Lynne had a cat," said Shirley. "She liked pets. Curtis didn't. 'Animals,' he would say, 'what can they do for you?' The cat's litter box was in the basement, and while she was away he would close the basement door to keep the kit-kat from using it. Sooner or later the cat would pee on the upstairs carpet, and then Curtis would have a reason to hurt it. She finally brought the cat over here to keep him away from it."

Each of these incidents by themselves are particularly disturbing and fit the classic abuser model, but, when combined to make a total picture, they show a personality that is insecure and controlling at best, criminally psychotic at worst.

THIRTY-ONE

In the spring of 1993, Lynne Matchem-Thomas was in the process of cracking up. While under the care of a psychiatrist, she was trying to work and carry several credit hours at University of Missouri-St. Louis. It was a time of alternating hope and despair — the fights with Curtis reaching a new level of volatility, the new budding romance with Martin. Everything seemed to be happening at once. Moving out from Curtis. Becoming independent. Trying to break in to the field of computer science. There were problems and complications at every turn.

All she had to help her get through this dark chapter of life was a mess of prescription drugs, supposed to make her mind right, keep her sane. She couldn't remember all their names, but their shapes and colors certainly stuck in her mind. Pink ovals, green tablets, orange capsules, white round ones. Put them all together and they looked real pretty, like movie-house candy, Chiclets or Ike & Mike, the kind she used to gobble as a kid in the darkness of the theater. But you had to be careful with these pills, how you took them — in what order, at what times of day, some with food, some with no dairy products, some with a big glass of water. She had a hard time keeping it all straight.

Maybe it happened because she didn't exactly follow the instructions on the prescription containers, or maybe the pills were just not right for her, but she had a bad reaction. For a couple of days in March, she had even been confined to a locked ward in Barnes Hospital. What a bringdown that was!

Lynne started seeing Dr. Elliot Nelson, a psychiatrist at Barnes Hospital, in November, 1992. She had been referred from a Dr. Pew, who, like Dr. Nelson, was a psychiatrist on the faculty of Washington University's School of Medicine. Pew's impression of the patient was "general social phobia with depressive features." Nelson amended this to a diagnosis of "adjustment disorder with depressed mood," though it still fell under the umbrella category of social phobia.

Social phobia, as Nelson would explain, is an anxiety disorder where a person may have particular difficulties with a certain social situation or possibly a number of social situations. Where it is normal to have some fear of public speaking, individuals with social phobia may dread it so much that they will take an F in class rather than speak out. They may curtail eating or drinking before going out in public for fear they will have to use a public restroom.

According to the intake report, Lynne's chief complaint was "panic attacks." She told Nelson that the attacks were brought on when she was under public scrutiny and that she had been avoiding social settings such as meetings and dinners with friends. Her symptoms during these episodes included abdominal discomfort, tightness of the chest, tremors, racing heartbeat and feeling flush and sweaty.

She described herself as a social drinker and a casual user of marijuana. She reported sleeping only four hours a night. She had lost her energy and her ability to concentrate. She was depressed, and her marriage was a big part of it.

"Patient reports severe marital problems," wrote Dr. Nelson in his report. "She describes a turbulent marriage and ... believes the relationship will terminate in divorce."

Nelson prescribed Zoloft, an anti-depressant in the same broad family as Prozac. Once that began to take effect, she would want to gradually put herself back in these social situations. If or when the anxiety symptoms appeared she should not run off but rather try to stay in the situation, attempting to tolerate them. If she could do that repeatedly, the anxiety should eventually subside and she could get her normal life back. It was a good plan with a history of proven results, but in Lynne's case it was only striking at the branches of the problem. The root cause was living with her.

When she returned on January 27, 1993, she reported side effects with the medication. She mentioned an inability to achieve orgasm (with Curtis, presumably) — a condition which Dr. Nelson noted was not uncommon with Zoloft — and some annoying spells of insomnia. Otherwise she was doing better. She hadn't had a full panic attack in a month or so. Nelson increased the Zoloft dosage and added a new prescription, Trazodone, an anti-depressant used for helping people sleep.

Then came the full-blown psychotic episode. On

March 6, Lynne was working as a teller at United Postal Savings. According to her mother, in the afternoon she began calling and saying strange things such as, "Call the operator and tell her to call you." Concocting an explanation that she was going to be given a lot of furniture and that she needed a trailer to move it, she asked that the family rent a U-Haul.

Lynne's behavior that day worried her supervisor to the point where he called her family and asked that someone come take her home. Her brother picked her up, and on the way home Lynne asked him to stop at Walgreen's. At the counter Lynne set down a six-pack of Michelob, a *Penthouse* and a birthday card for Curtis, though his birthday was three months away. Then, she tried to pay for it all with a check-cashing card from a local grocery chain.

She had dinner at her mother's, and afterward sat around drinking beer and talking. By evening, she was acting "different," recalled Shirley Matchem — restless, jittery, saying such crazy things that they took her to the emergency room at Barnes Hospital.

The attending psychiatric resident, Dr. Stacey Smith, examined the patient.

"Says she has weird blurred vision," Smith wrote in her clinical report. "When I asked her if she was seeing anything funny, she says, 'Oh yes, rabbits and birds flying around.' Says she hears grouchy voices telling her to be nervous, telling her to hurt herself. A boy voice commands her to hurt others. When you ask her if she has any thoughts of hurting herself or others, she totally denies it and laughs, wondering why I am asking that question."

She also thought she was having a baby.

"She says mother brought her here to have the baby," Smith noted. "She later stated: 'After you become pregnant, it takes two days for the baby to come out,' and asks, 'Am I having a boy?'"

Dr. Nelson did not see Lynne that day, but having been apprised of her symptoms by Dr. Smith he was certain that her behavior and hallucinations were precipitated by one or both of the anti-depressant drugs. The condition was termed Bipolar Disorder III, and it describes persons who only have psychotic episodes in response to anti-depressant medication. The plan agreed upon by Nelson was to admit Lynne to 15500 "with full precautions." Fifteen-five hundred is a locked ward where violent or dangerous or suicidal patients are confined.

Lynne was sinking deeper into the abyss. Mental illness cloaked her like a shroud. It is not important what she did or thought about during her two-day stay in 15500. What is important and worth mentioning is that this scared, confused person in the padded cell was certainly not the vivacious young woman who liked to roller blade and attend musicals at the Muny Theatre in Forest Park, who loved to read and was learning French. Nor was this the ambitious woman who had dropped out of high school, then gotten her GED and enrolled at the University of Missouri at St. Louis, working toward a career, a life of her own. This was somebody who was unraveling from the combined effects of a manic-depressive disease and an unhealthy living situation — and she was feeling more alienated by the day.

During her stay in 15500, the suspect drugs were discontinued, and she was put on Haldol. She responded quite well to that, reported Dr. Nelson. Haloperidal or Haldol is an anti-anxiety drug prescribed for treatment of psychotic states, most commonly schizophrenia. As of 1994 there were 13 chemically different anti-psychotic agents on the U.S. market, Haldol being the No. 1 prescribed anti-psychotic.

But Haldol may, and often does, produce unsettling side effects such as akathisia, a condition marked by extreme agitation and restlessness. People with episodes of akathisia have described the experience as a feeling of "screaming inside" and "jumping out of one's skin." Dr. Winston W. Shen, a psychiatrist with Saint Louis University School of Medicine, writing in the *Journal Of Nervous And Mental Disease*, notes that "akathisia is more difficult to endure than any of the symptoms for which the patient was originally treated." It is so discomforting that in certain South American countries authorities use Haldol to induce akathisia in prisoners, a form of torture which Amnesty International has roundly decried.

The drug Cogentin relieves the side effects of Haldol. Lynne was given a prescription for Cogentin and was supposed to have been taking both medications daily. After a month, however, she was back in Nelson's office asking to be put back on Zoloft. Despite the fact that he supposed her manic symptoms were triggered by the anti-depressant, Nelson complied.

———◆◆◆———

On at least two visits, starting in April, Lynne was accompanied by a tall, thin man whom she introduced to Dr. Nelson as her boyfriend. His name was Martin Plummer and she had known him for all of 10 days. During Lynne's session, Plummer would sit in the waiting room, reading magazines or gazing out the windows. Meanwhile, in the privacy and comfort of his office, Lynne propped herself on a plush leather sofa and spilled her soul to Nelson.

She had already mentioned her troubled family history, how she wasn't aware of her biological father until she was 13 and didn't meet him until she was 16, only to discover he was not very interested in her. And her mother, what a piece of work she was, always nervous and yelling. She wouldn't be surprised, she told Nelson, if Shirley was senile or even mentally ill. Growing up, her home life had been stressful. With her father not around, Lynne confided, Shirley had dated a number of men. Some of them were perverts and had tried to molest Lynne, even as early as five years of age. It had happened at least three different times, she said, though in each instance she was able to thwart the attempt.

Now, she had found her true soul mate. Martin was very supportive, very caring, and she wanted to pursue a serious relationship with him. He was a strong person, too, and she liked a strong person. A strong, *caring* person. Certainly not a strong, *un*-caring person like Curtis. And as for that bridge, it was burned. There was a major personality conflict between Curtis and her that had been stewing for years. They were on the brink of divorce. The only reason she had any contact with him was out of hope that he would continue paying her insurance premiums. She needed to get her anxiety disorder under control, she stressed to Nelson, before the divorce.

THIRTY-TWO

Dr. Elliot Nelson met Curtis' stare dead-on as he testified from the witness stand. Nelson was telling Dobrinic and the jury that Lynne had told him she was in love with Martin Plummer and was ending her marriage with Curtis. Moreover, he described Curtis as "very controlling" and said Curtis would phone him after his wife's visits asking him for details not only of his wife's treatment but of her confidences as well. Referring to his notes, he said that on April 23, 1993, Curtis had inquired whether Lynne had been unfaithful.

"What was your response to that?" asked Kathryn Dobrinic.

"When I would tell him that based on her wishes I could only give him the most basic information about his wife's treatment, he would then tell me that he was paying for her medical care through his insurance and he had a right to know."

Curtis worked in the mental-health system, so his clinical interest was understandable, yet he knew better than to inquire of his wife's psychiatrist whether she was sleeping around, and he was rebuffed every time he tried. Still, his curiosity was intense as well as his pride wounded. Curtis somehow knew about Plummer, and even though Curtis himself was as monogamous as a sultan, he absolutely hated the thought of playing the cuckold.

Dobrinic wanted Nelson's recollection of contact with the defendant on certain dates. "Checking my notes," said the doctor, "I had a call from Curtis Thomas on April 15, 1993. He was very concerned about Lynne's drinking in conjunction with her medication. He denied that she was having any manic symptoms, however he did state that he felt she was having an affair and that he put her out of the house."

As for her alcoholic intake, Lynne had described herself to Nelson as a social drinker, having just two beers a night; but any beer drinker will see the understatement there. Beer drinkers don't stop at two. Four or five maybe, but two is just a tease. It doesn't quite get you where you want to be. Never mind that Zoloft, the anti-depressant she was taking, was contraindicated by alcohol.

"Did you hear from him later that month?" queried Dobrinic.

"I spoke with him next, I believe, on the 22nd of April. He was concerned that Lynne was again having some symptoms of mania, and, because of this, he needed to talk to me urgently."

"What, if anything, occurred at that time?"

"I saw her the next day," replied the doctor, "and she

was in fact having some symptoms of mania. She had been feeling kind of hyper. She was sleeping less. She was more distractible. She reported increased sexual thoughts and impulsive sexual behavior, and she was feeling, to some degree, that she had special abilities to read other people's thoughts. This was all very atypical for her."

"Now, what did you attribute this development to?"

"Unfortunately, it seemed to be a clear return of symptoms of mania in response to the Zoloft. I had warned her that this might occur if we restarted it, but she felt the benefit was substantial enough that she wanted to take that chance."

Dr. Nelson said he decided to stop the Zoloft at that time and started her back on a very low dose of Haldol, again accompanied by the side-effect counteractant Cogentin. There was a prescription of Depakote, an anti-convulsant also used for treatment of manic episodes, thrown into the mix as well. With her medicine and dosages changing every three weeks, how could she get regulated? Lynne was really hopscotching around the pharmaceutical playground.

Dobrinic directed Nelson to April 30 and the upshot of that session. Lynne described the interaction she had with Curtis Thomas, remarked Nelson.

"And what interaction was that?"

"It occurred a few days before when she met with him at a restaurant. She stated that she was driving a rental car and he asked her for a ride. At some point they began to scuffle in the car, and he bit her on the arm, pushed her out of the car and actually drove off with this car she had rented."

Dobrinic directed Nelson to recall the 5th of May.

Did he have contact with either the defendant or Lynne? With both, he replied.

He didn't know whether it was before or after Lynne's appointment, but Curtis, he said, left a message with his secretary to call him. "When I called, he again demanded to know what was going on with Lynne's medical care. He stated, quote, that 'I have paid for her treatment.' I again told him that I could only give very cursory information as to comply with her wishes. He also asked about the Haldol. He was concerned about her drinking on the medication."

If Zoloft was contraindicated by alcohol consumption, Haldol, a much more potent drug, was doubly so.

Now, about that last session with the patient?

Nelson, speaking so rapidly the court reporter often had to stop him so she could catch up, said that when he had seen her on May 5, the day she disappeared, she was very much improved. She was sleeping well, concentrating well, her appetite was good. She said her father had been diagnosed with lung cancer and she was hoping to visit him in New York City.

"As per Mr. Thomas' concern, she denied drinking heavily and reported six beers over the last week. She denied manic symptoms of impulsivity, denied any feelings of special abilities or powers or any increase in religious or sexual thoughts — also symptomatic of mania," he added. She reported her marital situation was problematic, but she was doing so well otherwise that I made a decision to discontinue the Haldol."

"And why did you do that?"

"It was no longer necessary to continue her on an anti-psychotic, because her manic symptoms were completely resolved," replied the doctor.

"And when you described her marriage as being 'problematic,' what did you mean by that?"

"She was still telling me she had every intention of divorcing Curtis and pursuing the relationship with Martin Plummer."

"Did you see Lynne after that at any time?"

"No, I did not."

"Now, on May 7th, 1993, did anyone contact you concerning her?"

"Yes, I received phone calls from a female friend of Lynne's and also from her mother."

"And what did they inform you?"

"I was very shocked to hear that Lynne had not been seen by anyone since the appointment with myself two days earlier."

"Go on."

"They both expressed to me concerns that something horrible may have happened, that she may have actually been the victim of foul play from the defendant."

"Did you receive contact from anybody on May 10th?"

"I spoke with Martin Plummer on that day," said Nelson. "He told me he had not seen or heard from Lynne since before her last appointment. He was very worried and said he had been in close contact with the family ..."

"Let me ask you this," Dobrinic broke in, "did you have any contacts with the defendant after this?"

"I had numerous contacts with the defendant after this."

Nelson explained that Curtis called to talk about Lynne's disappearance. No, he did not have a specific date for this phone call, but he was certain it was within a week of Lynne's last appointment.

"What, if anything, did he say?"

Again, Nelson fixed Curtis in his gaze. Curtis stared right back. "He said that on May 5th Lynne called him from the hospital saying that her brother was late in picking her up and she wondered if he could come get her. He agreed, he said, but when he came to the office she wasn't there. But then he stated that he later saw her, that she stopped by his house at five-thirty and there they had argued over some money and some shoes that she had gotten from Martin. He said that the last he saw of her she was walking west on Waterman Avenue."

"Now, what, if any, reaction did you have to this phone call?"

"I was very surprised and concerned. I'd heard from the detective prior to that, that she had actually seen Mr. Thomas after the appointment. And so it was somewhat disconcerting for me to receive his call, because I ... had my own concerns about the nature of their relationship."

"What are those concerns?" asked Dobrinic expectantly.

Looking straight at the defendant, Nelson said, "I knew that there had been a lot of discord and violence between them, and I was worried that he may have been involved in her disappearance or that he may have killed her."

THIRTY-THREE

When Conroy had at him, we learned how very pedantic the young, handsome Dr. Nelson could be. He was the kind of maddening witness that has difficulty answering a question simply and directly. Instead, he strove to show the entire cause and effect: Ask him what time it is, he'd tell you how to build a clock. There seemed to be a natural enmity between Conroy and Nelson, the former being corrected like a schoolboy over his use of certain psychiatric terms and the latter finding out how very unpleasant cross-examination can be.

Conroy was attempting to play up the severity of Lynne's psychosis, planting the notion in the juror's minds that, despite her physician's claim that she was improved, she was still quite mentally ill and subject to wayward behaviors such as sexual promiscuity, which obviously might imperil her. Indeed, Nelson readily admitted that in the weeks prior to her death Lynne displayed "bizarre, disorganized behavior" such as jump-

ing out of a moving car, believing that she had tele-
pathic powers and brawling with another woman in an
East St. Louis bar, a tussle which earned her seven
stitches.

It was unusual, bordering on sensational, to have
testimony from a murder victim's psychiatrist, and
Conroy was going to take it to its fullest advantage.
First, he would demonstrate Curtis' genuine anxiety
over his wife's deteriorating condition. Holding a sheaf
of copied documents, the doctor's notes, Conroy
referred Nelson to April 22, 1993: "Now, on that day
you had a message from Curtis?"

Nelson glanced at his original notes and affirmed
this. "And the message was," Conroy continued, "that
Lynne's condition was worsening, and he told you this
was urgent, correct?"

"Right," replied Nelson.

"Would you read what your notes underneath the
word 'urgent' were that day."

"That there is a question of mania or hypomania.
And I have written 'grandiosity' — she was talking
about buying houses — 'decreased interest in sleep' and
'questioning whether she might be hypersexual' at that
time."

"Were Mr. Thomas' actions in that call to you consistent with those of a concerned husband?"

"If you could define 'concerned' ..."

Conroy dismissed the request with a wave of his
hand. "And now, referring to the day of April 23rd,
1993, she had an office appointment with you that day,
correct?"

Yes, said Nelson, the visit had been rescheduled
from the day before. "And you said that numerous

phone calls from *both* Curtis and Lynne's mother had preceded that appointment, correct?" Yes, replied Nelson. "And they reported their strong concerns that the patient was having manic symptoms?"

Nelson told how Shirley had reported hiding Lynne's Zoloft — she knew what it was doing, addling the poor girl — but that Lynne would find it. Also, how Lynne had some special power to know others' thoughts and was actually predicting what people would say before they said it.

Curtis, too, ever vigilant, had expressed grave doubts about Lynne's welfare. Conroy pressed Nelson to repeat for the record how Curtis had phoned him that day, mentioning not only her worsening mania but also broaching what he, Curtis, considered binge drinking and alcoholic blackouts. And there was a good possibility, Curtis added, that she was sleeping around.

"Was Mr. Thomas' behavior in that call to you indicative of a concerned husband?"

"I think you need to ask the question more specifically," replied Nelson.

"Again, doctor," said Conroy testily, "I am looking for a straight answer. Did it look like he was concerned about his wife?"

"My straight answer," replied the doctor, equally irritated, "is that at times he seemed concerned, and at times he seemed very rigid, very controlling and I couldn't separate out how much of which was going on."

"Going to the notes of your office appointment April 27th. Would you describe Mr. Thomas' assessment of Lynne as accurate on or about the 22nd of April?"

"Yes, quite accurate. He was right, she was having more manic symptoms."

"And this is two weeks before she was killed?"

Yes, from Nelson.

"And she was spending time with Martin Plummer during this period?"

Yes, from Nelson. From what she had said, they had been dating since the second week of April.

"Would you please read what you have written in your notes about that relationship."

Nelson complied, reading, "'She is currently involved in a relationship of 10 days, feeling she is very much in love,' but that she 'also had an impulsive sexual encounter with another individual.'"

At this, Curtis' ears seemed to prick up. He had been aware of her rutting around with more than one guy, and it pissed him off when he first learned of it, sure. But now, this coming out in court was sweet music to his ears. Conroy paused as Curtis leaned over to whisper something. He was quite involved with directing his own defense.

"By this 'individual,' I assume you are not referring to Martin Plummer with whom she was, quote: 'very much in love with?'"

"That is correct."

"Well then, who was it?"

The doctor had no idea. His notes on this matter were achingly sparse.

If he was going to win the case, Pat Conroy was going to have to drag the victim's character through the mud. "Now," he asked dryly, "is that consistent with mania, living with someone who you just met and having another sexual relationship at the same time?"

Dr. Nelson gave a tentative yes to that question and then launched into a bunch of gobbledygook about how it was difficult to gauge whether sleeping around was a result of her mania, whether she had true feelings for Plummer and so on.

"That's not what I asked," snapped Conroy. "Is that consistent?"

"As I said, sir, hypersexuality is a symptom of mania, that's certainly one, yes ..."

OK, he had shown that Lynne was a bit of a trollop, but that it was likely due to the medication and not a character flaw. And he had planted the notion that Curtis was really a peach of a guy, just wringing his hands over the whole unfortunate, out-of-control situation. Now, Pat Conroy would attempt to show that Lynne was a danger to herself and should never have been at large on the streets at the time of her disappearance.

He referred Nelson to his notes of April 23. Would he please read, starting with the eighth line down?

"'Patient's family decided she needed to be in the hospital and attempted to take her to the ER last night.'"

"Go on."

"They initially told her that they were going there for her brother, and then when they arrived they tried to have her register. She refused. When they drove her back home she attempted to jump out of the car several times."

"Go on."

"She reports that she just wanted to get away from them, that she was not trying to harm herself."

"Now, in addition to the patient telling you this, the

family also informed you that she tried to jump out of the car?"

"That is correct. That's why I offered her hospitalization. Among other reasons."

"And did the family accept this offer?"

"There was not enough insurance to cover an indefinite hospital stay, though the family did bring up the request that she be involuntarily committed."

"Continue."

"I explained that under Missouri law I felt she did not meet the requirements to be involuntarily committed, and both patient's husband and mother were understanding about this."

"What are the requirements?"

"To be immediately harmful to yourself or to others. Or, to be unable to provide for your basic needs of food, clothing, shelter. And you also have to have a mental illness."

"You don't think jumping out of a moving automobile is potentially harmful to someone?"

Nelson bristled. "While jumping out of a moving automobile is potentially harmful, Missouri commitment laws are such that you have to be *imminently* harmful to yourself or others."

"Hmm. So, the person needs to be tottering on the brink of destruction. Still, jumping out of a car could lead to ..."

"It depends on how fast the car was going, what the circumstances were, that sort of thing ..."

Nelson seemed quite perturbed at Conroy's imputation that his bad judgment had kept Lynne on the street when she should have been committed.

"And did you view Lynne as cured on her final visit

to your office?"

"In psychiatry, we never view anyone as cured. We talk about illness as being in remission. Her manic symptoms were in remission on May the 5th."

Lynne's health insurance was not the most comprehensive. In fact, at the end it had ceased to cover the visits. Conroy used this to prick the good doctor. Funny how his judgment that she no longer needed treatment coincided with the insurance money running out. In fact, when that happened, didn't he, Dr. Nelson, gallantly offer Lynne money to help pay for the needed medication?

She had improved, Nelson insisted. She was functioning much better in social situations, but she still needed her medicine, and, yes, he did offer to help pay the cost of her prescription, as a humanitarian gesture.

And after his grueling day on the stand, the doctor himself would likely need a dose of something. Can psychiatrists write their own prescriptions?

THIRTY-FOUR

That night in his cell Curtis was more pensive than usual. Normally he read for an hour or so before lights out. The selection in the prison library was insultingly narrow in scope. There was no doubt that cowboy writer, Louis L' Amour, was the hands-down favorite among this population. There was a whole long shelf of dog-eared L' Amour paperbacks, all of them with a variation of some squinty-eyed, rifle-toting buckaroo on the cover. Looked like the fucking Marlboro Man. As if he gave a rat's ass about some cowboy's problems.

Then there were a few shelves of novels dating mostly to the '60s and '70s. Authors such as John Jakes and James Michener — historical stuff with just a tease of cheesecake about every 60 pages: "The sweat glistened on her heaving breasts ..." Shit like that. You couldn't have any reading material that might arouse the prurient interest of the cell block, or the laundry people would bitch that the sheets were too funky. Talk about writers, he mused, in St. Louis there were famous writers living just a few blocks from his house. William

Gass for one. A great writer, so he'd heard. He never actually read his stuff. Howard Nemerov, the Wash U. prof and poet laureate of the United States in his later years, used to walk down the Delmar Loop and stop in his newsstand for a copy of the Sunday *New York Times* with the literary supplement inside. Once Nemerov showed him a review that he'd written. He seemed to want to show it to somebody, and Curtis was there. It was talking about some other poet's new book. Curtis made a comment about mutual masturbation in the literary world, and Nemerov seemed to take it in the spirit it was meant — as a joke. He was an all right guy, Nemerov, but he was dead now.

But Curtis didn't want fiction or poetry. He wanted meaningful biography — as a young man he had devoured Claude Brown's *Manchild In The Promised Land*. He could relate to that book even more now, he thought wryly. He was doing time just like Claude Brown did time, and for that matter just like Eldridge Cleaver, like Nelson Mandela, like Martin Luther King Jr., like Malcolm X. Of course, they had been in the joint for political crimes, nothing even remotely akin to the crime he was accused of, decapitating his wife. Still, a socially conscious black man doing time was a noble thing, right?

And he wanted intelligent discussion of social issues, *Black Reconstruction,* for example, by the great W.E.B. DuBois. That was the good stuff, and the only way he was ever going to get enrichment like that was to have someone buy it at the bookstore and mail it to him. Maybe Bufus or Bennie would spring for it. His brothers sure ought to do *some*thing for him. They hadn't even been up here to visit, not one goddam time in six months — but what was he thinking? He was going to be out of here early next week.

Or was he? He shuddered to think of five years or more in prison. God, what a waste! He couldn't let that happen, but the awful thing was the events were now out of his control. If it was going to happen, if he was going to do *real* time, it would be because of those Judases at Independence Center who had testified, *eagerly* it seemed, making up shit that either never happened or didn't happen when they said it happened. And it would be because of people like Nelson, the pompous asshole, telling the court, "Oh, I was worried that he may have been involved in her disappearance or that he may have killed her."

Unbelievable, having an expert witness testify to the guilt of the defendant. What bullshit! But bullshit that could actually put him away.

He was in a most precarious perch, and his life had come to this because of so many reasons.

He had been edged out of his bid for student-body president at Wash U.

He had to fold his newsstand at St. Louis Centre after the leasing office raised the rent.

He had married a crazy woman, and he had taken up with another woman even crazier than his wife.

He couldn't get the SBA loan he needed to buy the Ambassador Theatre and turn it into a nightclub.

He'd been unjustly fired from several good jobs.

The cops and prosecutors just didn't like him.

And to top it all off he had been born black. Not that he would want to be anything else. Black was cool in almost every circumstance except for what was now happening to him in this redneck county.

THIRTY-FIVE

April 1993 had been a stormy month for Lynne. She had lost her job because of alternating grandiosity and incoherency stemming from the side effects of the drugs she was taking. She was also trying to move out from Curtis, but he was making it hard. During one visit around mid-month, Lynne told Dr. Nelson that when she had gone to the Waterman residence to get her clothes, Curtis first criticized her wardrobe and then "begged and pleaded with her to come back to him."

Later in the month, Lynne returned to collect her belongings, this time with her sister-in-law, Michelle. They let themselves in with a key that Lynne had secreted and were boxing things up when Curtis came in unexpectedly. Lynne hid under the stairs. Curtis, already on a short fuse because of Lynne's endearment for Martin Plummer, was furious at the perceived home invasion. Of Michelle, he demanded an explanation, and when he got it he responded by summarily forbidding the removal of any of Lynne's things. Curtis and

Michelle then got into it, which prompted Lynne to emerge from her hiding place. The three of them fought in the foyer: Michelle was shoved to the floor, Curtis was scratched on the face and Lynne had her arm jammed against a door. The women ran out and called 911.

"This has got to stop," said the responding officers to Lynne and her sister-in-law. They were at the Central West End Savings and Loan at the corner of Waterman and DeBaliviere; the guard there had made the call. The 9th District cops felt warranted in their chastisement. How many times had they responded to an 84, a domestic disturbance, at the Waterman address in the last five years? Three, or was it four?

"There's an old saying," said the older cop to Lynne. "You've either got to fish or cut bait. We can't always be here when you need us or as fast as you need us. So you've got to work out these differences with your husband. Go to a marriage counselor for crissake! Or get away from him once and for all."

"That's what I'm *trying* to do," said Lynne, exasperated.

———◆◆◆———

The incident at St. Mary's Hospital was the final crushing blow to their marriage. During the last week of April, Lynne had rented a car to help move her stuff. She wrote a check to Costello Leasing and drove off the lot in a new Chevy Cavalier. These car rental places must be able to access a person's checking account in a matter of hours, for when Curtis came home from work that day there was a message on his answering machine from Costello urging Lynne to return the car. When Curtis called the agency, a woman told him the check bounced and stressed that the car must be brought back.

Curtis phoned Shirley's home and Lynne answered. He told her about the problem with the rental agency, and she denied insufficient funds. Her balance was $500 or more, she said. They agreed to meet at Redel's restaurant and talk it out. Curtis got there at six, as agreed, but there was no Lynne. Typical, thought Curtis, growing more irked by the minute. He bought a Bud and sat at the bar, looking at Lee Redel's antique camera collection displayed in little nooks here and there. Finally, Lynne walked in. She looked good, he had to admit, hair all done up, nice print dress, a little cleavage showing. Walking up to him at the bar, it was almost like old times, and he forgot for a moment how goddam irritated he was with her.

They sat talking about their truly screwed-up marriage, and Curtis mentioned he had a manic-depressive support meeting at St. Mary's Hospital. He was only doing it to be able to cope with her strange behavior as of late, so for all the trouble she'd put him through would she at least give him him a ride in the rental?

They drove to St. Mary's and, once there, parked in the circle drive at the entrance, it got ugly with the shouting and hitting and clawing and biting. Two men standing outside saw it happen. One of them was Wade Faraone, whose mother had undergone kidney surgery that morning. Faraone and his stepfather needed a smoke, and that's what they were doing outside, smoking and chatting idly. Two-and-a-half years later,

I may be wanted for assault...and car theft too

Faraone would be on a witness stand in an Illinois courtroom, testifying about the altercation that April evening.

Dobrinic asked, "Now, while you were outside, what, if anything, did you see?"

Faraone began, "When we was standing there, there was an empty parked car sitting right in the circle drive. And then a lady, a black lady, walked out of the hospital, walked to the car, got in and started it. She hadn't even closed the door yet when a black gentleman ran from behind, came up to the car and an argument started."

Go on, said Kathryn Dobrinic. "Well," drawled the witness, "she managed to get the car into drive and was barely moving when the guy threw himself across her lap and must've put the car into park. He punched her, like four or five times in the face and head, and backed off. Then, he drug her from the car, and I believe her purse came out with her, and he jumped into the car and took off."

Faraone related how he helped the lady get her purse together, how he walked her into the hospital's reception area and "the only thing she said was that her boyfriend really wanted the car and that was what the fight was about."

At the request of the prosecutor, Faraone then identified Curtis as the "boyfriend."

Curtis kept the car overnight. The next day, he drove the car to the courts building downtown to file for divorce. When he got back home there was another message saying the car needed to be returned by 1 p.m that day. The woman sounded like if the company could just get the car back everything would be forgiven. Curtis took back the car and then turned himself in to the police.

They didn't even have to sweat him down. Curtis calmly strolled into the Richmond Heights stationhouse and presented himself to Detective Mark Tackes. "I may be wanted for assault ... and car theft too," he announced. And he was right. Tackes Mirandized him and informed him he could have an attorney present. But Curtis declined, acting contrite enough to impress the detective, saying he realized that what he did was wrong and he just wanted to get it off his chest.

Sitting in an interview room with bare walls, he composed an official statement about the incident.

" ... Lynne went around to the driver's side and wedged herself in between the door and the seat," he wrote. "We struggled, and I bit her. I took control of the car and proceeded to drive away at 10 to 15 miles per hour with Lynne hanging on the door, which was part way open. After 10 to 20 feet, Lynne fell off, and I stopped the car, observed her for injury and continued home."

He forced her out of a moving car, but hey, at least he observed her for injury.

Curtis concluded his statement with the lame justification that "my actions were prompted by the illness Lynne is currently going through."

Costello had their rental back with only a few dings and dents. They decided to let it go. Lynne was humiliated by the incident, yet she declined to press charges for assault. Curtis skated on that one, but the ice was getting thinner.

PART IV

THIRTY-SIX

Curtis had a thing for women and libraries. He had met his wife in a college library, and he met Deborah Claybrook in the main public library in downtown St. Louis. Deborah put that first meeting back around 1982. Eventually, they started dating, but for one reason or another it didn't work out. The years went by. Curtis got married, and Deborah moved to Edwardsville, Illinois, to attend the university there.

Deborah Claybrook returned to St. Louis in the summer of 1992, and it was sometime after that when Curtis saw her name and phone number on a sign-up sheet for a volunteer organization. He called her in mid-April 1993 to say hello and catch up on things. They made a date to meet at Redel's, the site of Curtis and Lynne's frequent dinings-out. It was the first time they had seen each other in five years.

Was it by design or coincidence that the next time

they met was on May 5? Curtis called her at the Regional Commerce & Growth Association, the city's Chamber of Commerce, where she was a clerical temp. She had offered to help him with a cover letter for an employment query, and he wondered whether she would drop by after work so they could go over it.

When Deborah Claybrook drove up to Curtis' house about 5:45 p.m. she saw a woman on the porch and Curtis standing in the doorway talking to her. By the time she made a U-turn and parked, the woman was standing on the sidewalk as if waiting to meet her. She wore green pants and a striped top. The sandals and the backpack slung over her shoulder made Deborah think the woman was a student. Deborah started tentatively up the walk toward the house.

"Hello," said the woman, not unfriendly. "I'm Lynne, Curtis' ex-wife." She fibbed about the prefix "ex."

This revelation stung Deborah. Why, she wondered, would Curtis, obviously interested in her romantically, ask her over and have his ex-wife present? And why hadn't he mentioned being divorced while at Redel's the other night? They had talked about so many personal things.

Curtis came down to the sidewalk. He nodded to Deborah, but his attention was on the other woman. They were having words — not raising their voices really, but making threatening statements. Deborah heard Curtis mutter something she couldn't make out. Then she heard the woman say to Curtis, "You know I can hurt you. I can do some damage to you."

Deborah Claybrook stayed for just a few minutes and then drove off hurt and confused by the encounter. Heading east on Waterman she looked in her rearview

She drove off hurt and confused by the encounter

mirror at the receding scene; Curtis and Lynne were still on the sidewalk talking.

Without knowing it, Deborah Claybrook was becoming intricately involved in a murder. It's anybody's nightmare. You meet someone you think you like, you make the decision to spend time with that person, and they turn out to be evil. Oh, they hide it well in the beginning, but given enough time a sinister nature is bound to surface like a drowned body after three weeks in a cold, quiet lake.

Two days later, on a Friday evening, Deborah returned to Curtis' house. Since the ugly incident on Wednesday, he had called her several times and convinced her that the woman she'd met was an old girlfriend that he couldn't get rid of. At any rate, he indicated, it was definitely over between them. He was indeed available, a single guy. Deborah liked Curtis, and she didn't want to see their fresh romance wither on the vine, so she agreed to give it another shot. As it happened, however, that evening was the evening that Shirley Matchem and the two police officers dropped by Curtis' home to investigate a missing person. Deborah, thinking she was there for a candlelight dinner, instead found herself held up to scrutiny, literally, as the possible missing wife of her new boyfriend. The experience mortified her.

After Curtis called Herman Jimerson and stopped the search, and once the cops and Shirley had gone, he and Deborah sat and recounted the episode. Curtis refilled their glasses with good cabernet. He spilled his soul to her as he would several times over the course of the summer. Why were they doing this to him? That woman Lynne was so flighty, so incredibly unpredictable, she could be anywhere — holed up in some crack-house, shacking up with someone she'd met, or on a three-day bender in a series of Northside lounges.

Curtis swirled the cabernet in the glass and stared thoughtfully at the filmy residue it left. "It's a terrible thing," he murmured, "to have people think that you're a murderer."

In the eyes of the law, Deborah Claybrook was officially associated with Curtis. As Lynne's disappearance stretched on, detectives questioned Curtis several times. When they wanted to find him and could not, they came to her home looking for him.

Deborah heard a knock at the door of her parent's home. When she opened the door, there stood two serious-looking guys in sport coats. They introduced themselves as Detectives Reed and Montague with the St. Louis Police Department. They asked if they could come in and speak with her. It was Tuesday afternoon, the 18th of May, 1993.

They told her they wanted to talk to Curtis about his missing wife. Where was he? What could she tell them? Nothing, she insisted. She had only met the woman in passing, and for a few minutes. It could be big trouble, they stressed, for Curtis Thomas or *anyone involved with him* if the wife turned up a victim of foul play.

Despite being terribly flustered, Deborah tried to maintain her composure. She had only been reacquainted with Curtis Thomas for a few weeks, she informed the detectives, she didn't know much about his habits or his social life. But the detectives hung around and kept asking questions in a tone that made her think that maybe *she* was a suspect. It scared the hell out of her. As they were leaving, the one detective said that she may have to come down to the station and take a polygraph test.

Though she was being implicated, Deborah wasn't quite ready to believe that Curtis was a murderer. She continued seeing him.

THIRTY-SEVEN

As their relationship grew, Deborah began spending time at Curtis' house. It was nice to have another place to go besides her parent's home. Up until the 1970s the entire Southside had been predominantly white. Now the near Southside was liberally populated with black families, though the far Southside, the Scrubby Dutch neighborhoods down around St. Louis Hills and Carondelet, was still as white as a vanilla concrete at Ted Drewe's. Robert and Mary Claybrook's modest residence in the Carondelet neighborhood was an exception. The Claybrooks along with a couple of dozen other middle-class black households all clumped together comprised an ebony island amidst a sea of white. "Little Africa," folks called it. Most of those families had been there for generations. They were good citizens, productive and pleasant and, most importantly to the other Southsiders, they kept their property up.

To Deborah, the big, three-story brick house on Waterman was a world away from her own. The place intrigued her with all its secret nooks and strange props lying around. One day she had seen a woman's purse on the ground near the porch. Another day, in early May, she had seen a red gasoline can and bags of cement on the porch.

The rooms were filled with nice furniture, many of them antiques. There were hanging plants and handsome rugs, too. It was a comfortable feeling inside. On the fireplace mantle Curtis kept some newspaper articles, clipped from the *St. Louis Post-Dispatch*, about the murdered woman found in Litchfield. When she asked about them he said that he was interested in the case because the autopsy on that body showed a fibrous growth in the uterus. Lynne had fibroid tumors — the reason, he said, why they never had children. Anyway, it was just a coincidence about the tumors. This body up north was that of a white woman.

Curtis' comments were nonchalant and somewhat ambiguous. There was no real reason to think that the body in Litchfield and his estranged wife — he had finally told her the truth about that — were one and the same. That was idle speculation over those clippings, Deborah told herself, he was just thinking the worst. She had thought about that poor murdered girl in Litchfield. No one to claim her body. How sad. There had been a case like that in St. Louis back in the early '80s, a young decapitated girl, thought to be only 9 years old, found in a derelict building. They kept her body in the morgue for a long time, over a year, hoping someone would be able to identify her, but no one came forward, and, finally, they put her to rest. How, she wondered, could a human body, even without a head, fail to be identified? Somebody would just *have* to be missing that person. Why not take these Jane and John Does, compile their physical descriptions and the circumstances around finding their bodies, and run it on national TV like *America's Most Wanted?* That would probably get results.

But this body in Litchfield, why didn't Curtis follow his hunch instead of just dismissing it? If he even thought that there might possibly be a connection with Lynne, why didn't he bring it to the attention of the police? It certainly couldn't hurt. The fibroid tumor thing was coincidental, maybe too coincidental. And maybe they had the girl's race wrong. Maybe she wasn't a white girl at all, but a light-skinned black girl. That would explain it. Come to think of it, in her hazy recollection of Lynne, the woman *was* light-complexioned. What was going on? There was no way he ... he couldn't have, could he? A glimmer of doubt, incipient suspicion, seeped into her mind.

Deborah Claybrook had never been in trouble with the law. She had never had cause to seek a lawyer. Now she felt she needed one. Her mother was pressing her too. Just explain the situation and find out what rights you have, she urged. One day Deborah and her mother were in Schnucks supermarket near Carondelet Park when a blue booklet in the free racks caught their eye. They thumbed through *The St. Louis Legal Directory*, noting names and pictures of men and women attorneys along with descriptions of their areas of practice. The attorneys in the pictures were all smiling; they looked friendly enough. However, only one of the pictures showed an African-American attorney. His name was Herman Jimerson.

Jimerson came out to greet Deborah Claybrook in the reception area of the fourth-floor law offices in the upscale Bonhomme Place Building, in Clayton. Jimerson was about her age, late 30s — tall, slender and impeccably groomed. He led her down a hall and into his office. It had a nice view, she noted. "What can I do for you?" he asked politely as they sat.

Slowly, deliberately she told him about Curtis and about the police. Jimerson listened raptly, and when she was finished he told her he couldn't help her. He knew both Lynne and Curtis socially. In fact, Curtis had recently consulted him on the very matter she spoke of. It would be unethical, a breach of professional standards, for him to advise her, except that she might consider staying away from Curtis altogether until Lynne's disappearance was resolved.

Deborah Claybrook left, astounded that with the thousands of attorneys in the metro area she had picked the one whose hands were tied to help. She pursued it, however. She went to Legal Aid and laid out the situation before another lawyer: "This guy I'm seeing, his ex-wife is missing, and the police have questioned him and now me. They've been to my house. They've said I should take a lie-detector test. I'm scared. What can they do to me?"

In some cities "Legal Aid" is the public defender. In St. Louis, Legal Aid is Legal Services of Eastern Missouri, a free counseling service for those beset by legal problems of a civil nature only. And while nobody had been charged with anything yet, Deborah's predicament did not meet their criteria. All they could do was refer her to a private attorney. Been there, done that,

thought Deborah. For the time being, she would give
up on finding a lawyer.

⸺⸻•⸻⸺

Deborah continued seeing Curtis during May. She
would drive him to and from work, and sometimes they
just tooled around. On a Thursday, the last in May, she
picked up Curtis and they drove to the Southern
Illinois University campus in Edwardsville. As a student, Deborah had often walked the nature trail there.
It was one of her favorite places, and she wanted to
show it to her new lover. But as they stopped for gas
and she was outside at the pumps, she noticed Curtis
furtively going through her purse and rummaging in the
glove compartment. He never knew she saw him, and
she didn't say anything, though she couldn't understand why he would do something so strange.

Deborah Claybrook spent June with Curtis. It was a
very intense time, filled with hopes and fears and
recriminations. By July, however, the relationship was
spiraling down fast. On Independence Day, they went
to Berry Relder's house and Curtis was so cool toward
her that she couldn't help but think he was deliberately
trying to humiliate her. Two days after the Fourth they
went to the Eric Marenthal concert on Laclede's
Landing at the riverfront — even as the turgid waters
of the Mississippi began to first spill their banks and
become what would be called the Great Flood of '93.

Curtis loved Marenthal, considered him one of the
great exponents of jazz fusion, and as a present Deborah

She knew then that her boat had sailed

had bought tickets for them both. But as they stood in line to get in, Curtis started hitting on another woman. Deborah heard him asking for her phone number, not even trying to be sneaky about it, the bastard. She suddenly recalled what someone had told her about Curtis, a casual comment from a one-time acquaintance of his, though a warning nonetheless: "Curtis is a straight-up dog about women," the man had said.

She knew then that her boat had sailed. At one point she and Curtis had talked of her moving in with him, but how could that ever happen? He didn't appreciate her, especially now that he'd gotten a car and didn't need her to take him to work. He was always borrowing money, too. Nothing big — a dollar here, a five there, but what kind of guy never has any cash handy? Now he's flirting with strange women right in front of me. Time to move on, she reasoned. She turned her back on Curtis, Eric Marenthal and the mounting floodwaters and drove home.

THIRTY-EIGHT

The transcripts from the trial number 10 volumes, each volume some 250 pages in length. As trial transcripts go, it is a tome. Deborah Claybrook's testimony takes up an entire volume plus portions of two on either side of it. For two days during the trial she was washed, rinsed and hung out to dry.

A slightly pudgy woman, her jet hair pulled back in a tight bun, she spoke softly, distinctly from the witness stand in measured words, making sure to say what she wanted to say.

Under direct examination by Kathryn Dobrinic, she recounted that all that spring and summer the police were looking into Lynne's disappearance. Twice since the night of May 7, Deborah had been over to Curtis' home when the detectives came calling. She sat there and listened to their pressing, persistent queries, and even though Curtis was mum to the police, he began dropping hints of his involvement in the murder to her, growing more confessorial as time went on. One evening in late May or early June, after lovemaking, they were lying in bed, snuggled up against one another, when Curtis asked her what did she think had happened to Lynne. She replied that she thought he had murdered her.

"Why did you tell him that?" questioned Dobrinic.

"Because he had told me too many things that were related to the articles in the newspaper," replied Claybrook.

"And when you said that to the defendant, what was his response?"

"He got up and started pacing," she said, "and he started to tell me what actually had happened. He told me that shortly after I left that Wednesday that he had murdered Lynne and put her body in a box in the basement and that's why he didn't want the police to search there."

"Continue, Deborah."

"He also told me that he had cut off her head. At that point I told him to stop."

"Why?"

"Because it was getting too gory, all the details. But he kept on. He told me the body in Litchfield was Lynne's. He told me that, before he dumped the body, he put gasoline on it and when he lit it, her body ... he wasn't prepared for the bright flash, so bright it scared him."

"Did he make any comment to you about what he had done with the head of the body?"

"He told me all I needed to know was that he had

put the head in a bucket and covered it with cement and that it would never be found."

"What else did he tell you that night?"

"He said that with all the problems he was having with Lynne, he decided to get rid of her, that he had planned it and was waiting for the right time. That first time the police came to his house, he thought they would be back the next day with a search warrant. He thought he would wake up surrounded by police and he would be arrested. When the police didn't come and when the body was misidentified as a white woman, he knew that he had probably gotten away with it."

"What was your reaction?"

"I wanted him to tell me it wasn't true. I ... I didn't know whether to run screaming out of the house or what."

"You continued to see him?" Dobrinic pressed.

"Yes, I did."

"And how could you do that?"

Claybrook took a breath. "I don't really expect anyone to understand," she began, "but it's like I just couldn't believe that I knew someone who would do something so awful. I kept waiting for someone to tell me that this was true or it wasn't true."

"Did you love this man?"

"No, I did not."

"But you stayed with him?"

"I thought it would be in my best interest to befriend Curtis. I felt it was much easier to read his reactions and to know what he felt by being close to him, other than having him show up on my doorstep or at my job one day and not know what he was thinking. He told me he loved Lynne, but he murdered her. I believed Curtis liked me, but he could murder me as well."

"You did not go to the police?"

"No, I didn't. The papers said it was a white female. I had no proof the two were connected. What would make the police believe me?"

Dobrinic took a second to gaze at some spot on the wall, for dramatic effect perhaps, then returned to the questioning. "Did the defendant have any conversations with you about going to the police?"

"I had asked him would he turn himself in, and he laughed and said that he had gotten away with it. The police would never find out."

"What about your involvement?"

She had done all right until now, avoiding Curtis' glacial stare, but like Medusa's victims she ultimately could not resist looking. "He told me ..." She paused and seemed to stiffen. "... that if I did go to the police that he would involve me in the murder."

"Did you believe him?"

"Oh, yes I did," Claybrook shot back. "He told me that it was a matter of survival. He told me that he would bring his own mother down if it would save his life."

THIRTY-NINE

Twice while Claybrook was under direct examination, Conroy had asked to approach the bench, and in a sidebar requested that the witness' testimony be halted until she had undergone psychiatric evaluation. Too late for that.

" ... and it is the defense's position that this witness is mentally incompetent, has perjured herself, and, unless she can substantiate what she is talking about, I am putting for purposes of the record that this goes to her competency to testify ..."

Judge Huber mulled this over for about two beats and responded. "I have watched the demeanor of this witness. She seemed truthful. She has easily described what happened. I see no reason to order a psychiatric evaluation."

So Conroy thought Claybrook crazy as a bat. He had reason. Just in the past month, she had been the object of a police search, only to be found camped out in a car in the middle of a soybean field in Salem, Illinois.

People were after her. She had to escape.

Actually, there was nothing to prove that she was being followed. She had been mired in gobs of icky psychic residue from being with Curtis and it likely had left her paranoid. Still, there was a kernel of legitimacy to her concerns, because sometime after she and Curtis split up things began to get weird. For instance, she had this apartment in the city for a year-and-a-half, no problems, and then suddenly the landlord revoked her lease, gave her 20 days to move out. Too much noise, was the reason he gave. Then she accidentally sideswiped a car down the street, and so she put her name and phone number on the windshield. That prompted a series of strange phone calls, a man asking for a cash settlement, though, when Deborah pressed him, he didn't know the license number on the stricken car. Also, the address he gave as his own didn't pan out. The house was vacant.

Then came the thing with Alderick Reed. He was one of the two detectives who had come to her mother's house, the one who tried to coax her into taking a polygraph test. When Deborah Claybrook read the *St. Louis Post-Dispatch* on March 16, 1994, she got a start. Detective Reed and another officer, Bobby Baker, had been arrested by Clarence Harmon, the chief of police himself. They had been charged with extortion, allegedly for shaking down a motorist whom they had stopped. The guy had a concealed weapon and they supposedly let him go for a $300 bribe. The shakedown victim, a fellow named Scott Crawford, later decided that a possible concealed-weapons charge was worth seeing a couple bad eggs fry. He filed a formal complaint with the police department. (In twin verdicts that puzzle to this day, Reed would eventually be acquitted and Baker found guilty on state and federal charges).

Deborah Claybrook read the story and thought, hey, if this cop is corrupt, maybe the whole Lynne Thomas investigation was somehow rigged or falsified. Who knew what sort of agenda was in play? She had wondered why the police never returned to Curtis' home with a search warrant. Did this Reed have anything to do with that?

She had carried Curtis' confession around with her for more than a year now, the thing gnawing at her soul, until the investigation caught up with her again. When St. Louis homicide detectives Joe Nickerson and Joe Burgoon came to her in the fall of 1994, she was nothing but relieved. By then she had decided to make a stand in choosing to believe that Curtis did murder his wife. She would help the police as much as she could to convict him.

The detectives were reassuring — Nickerson had gone to school with her brother at St. Mary's High. Unlike Reed and Montague, they didn't come on like hard-asses, scaring her half to death. They told her it would be all right. In turn, she told them everything — all her fears, Curtis' confession, his threats. The detectives nodded sagely, they took notes. The next month, November, they shopped her story to the city prosecutors, but the assistant circuit attorney in the homicide unit, a young woman by the name of Deborah Van Arink, wasn't crazy about Claybrook or her tale. She told Claybrook that she could not in good conscience bring these allegations before a grand jury.

"You would be viewed as a disgruntled girlfriend," said Van Arink, "and in all likelihood your testimony would be thrown out of court." So, the case was taken under advisement, which meant that they were thinking about prosecuting it but not at the present.

Devastated, Deborah Claybrook left the Municipal Courts building, walking down the steps on to Market Street, and by the time she got to the statue of Ulysses S. Grant she was close to puking. Never had she felt so disenfranchised, so dumped on, so isolated. First the black lawyer refused to help and now the city prosecutors. It actually made her physically ill.

Burgoon and Nickerson didn't have a problem with Claybrook's story, however, and they weren't about to let it go. They again touted their case to the circuit attorney, and at the same time there was a nudge from up Hillsboro way.

"The next thing we knew about it," said St. Louis Circuit Attorney Dee Joyce-Hayes, "was the prosecutor up in Montgomery County called my Chief Trial Assistant, Shirley Rogers, and ran the situation by her. Shirley brought me in on it and I agreed with her as well as the detectives that the case should be given a second look."

So Deborah Claybrook came back, repeating the lurid details of the confession — telling it first to newly attentive prosecutors, then to a grand jury. Ultimately, she got her wish; the State brought its case against her ex-boyfriend and made her its primary witness.

FORTY

Herman Jimerson was brushing his teeth, getting ready for bed, when the phone rang. He hoped it wasn't a client. He didn't so much mind his clients calling him at home if it was important, and actually he gave out his number to many of them, but he didn't condone them calling after 10 p.m. He padded into the study and picked up the phone on its fourth ring. He said hello. The voice at the other end was halting, tentative.

"Mr. Jimerson? This is Deborah Claybrook. I came to you a couple years ago concerning the disappearance of a Lynne Matchem-Thomas. Well, I guess you know they identified her body, she'd been murdered. Decapitated and set on fire, just horrible ..."

"Yes, I know," said the attorney abruptly. "Why are you calling me now?"

"It's just that the trial is coming up next month and

I'm scheduled to testify, for the State, you know, and it seems I'm the only witness whose testimony is, like, direct evidence. I'm really putting myself out on a limb, you see? I feel like I'm crossing a desert on my own."

"What are you calling about?" he repeated. He didn't like this. She was pretty distraught. He would give her 10 seconds before he hung up.

"I told you things during our consultation," she said, "what Curtis told me. You seemed to believe me. You know Curtis. You know what he's capable of doing. You know he killed her because you stopped the police from going down the basement. If it weren't for you ..."

"You can stop right there," he cut in. Jimerson was growing suspicious by the moment, thinking that the call was being recorded, that it could be a trick to get some corroboration for her story. "Regardless of his guilt or innocence, I'm glad I gave Curtis that advice,

Why are you calling me now

because then I did my job as a lawyer."

She said, "How can you live with yourself, knowing what you know?"

"Look dear, it's not my case and not my problem. I'm telling you now what I told you then: You need to consult a lawyer, someone else besides me. Now goodbye."

Herman Jimerson stood there reflectively, the toothbrush still in his hand. The call had unnerved him, he had to admit. It wasn't as if he had ever put the matter out of his mind. No, he had mulled the whole thing over considerably, lost sleep over it, and he hated feeling as if he had to choose allegiances between two close friends — one slain, the other the accused slayer. One thing for sure, though Curtis might be responsible for pulling off any number of scams, he emphatically did not want to believe that Curtis killed Lynne. In fact, it sent his mind reeling to think Curtis would do something so horrific to somebody like her, a gorgeous woman so full of life. She was probably the best thing he ever had.

FORTY-ONE

Around noon of September 26, 1995, Deborah Claybrook told her mother she was going to walk her cat in the park. Five minutes later, the cat was outside scratching to get in the house, and the family car was gone. This was not at all like her to just drive off without saying anything. Maybe she went to work, thought her mother. Mary Claybrook waited awhile and called Incarnate Word Hospital, where Deborah had a clerical position. No, said the supervisor sounding altogether unconcerned, Deborah was not there. Her parents were frantic. Deborah was seeing a therapist, true, though even professional help didn't curb her fears. She had confided to her mother just the week before that she was convinced that people were following her, on foot and in cars, and that these people wanted to harm her. Now she was missing. Mary Claybrook picked up the phone and dialed 911.

The police and prosecutors connected to the case

were dyspeptic. Here was the State's key witness in a murder trial set to get underway in less than a month and she was missing. It was all over the 10 o' clock news, her parents pleading with the phantom abductors not to hurt her. Incidentally, very few missing persons are the subject of television news accounts, especially at the onset of their disappearance. Many TV stations have a policy against reporting about missing persons, fearing a hoax might be played. But in Claybrook's case the law stepped in.

"The police contacted us or else we never would have touched it," said Susan Edwards-Gold, a producer at KTVI Channel 2 in St. Louis.

She had driven to Salem "out of fear," she told Kathryn Dobrinic from the witness stand. Hoping to head Conroy off at the pass, Dobrinic had broached the subject of Deborah Claybrook's escapade. She would rather the jury hear the story under friendly persuasion. "Again," said Claybrook, "I felt that people were following me, and I was just so certain that someone would harm me and that no one would care. So I came to Illinois, and I drove into a soybean field to throw these people off, and I stayed there 'til I could clear my head."

Why Salem? Deborah claimed no connection with the old Illinois town on U.S. Highway 50, birthplace of famed orator and three-time presidential candidate William Jennings Bryan, just as Curtis claimed no connection with Litchfield. It was weird all right.

She spent three days and two nights in the soybean field doing Lord knows what. When they found her she was walking down the road looking for a town, having somehow locked herself out of her car. That's what she told the deputy who took her to the Marion County Sheriff's Department. It didn't take long to figure out that she was the missing state's witness, and the police in St. Louis were soon notified. Nickerson and Burgoon were dispatched to Salem to pick her up.

Both cops were seasoned homicide investigators, but Burgoon, lean and silver-haired, father of seven, belonged in the pantheon of the world's greatest detectives. Philip Marlowe, Mike Hammer and Miss Marple all had nothing on him. And with 35 years as a cop and homicide investigator behind him, he believed Deborah Claybrook's story. The way he saw it, she was a nice lady, came from a good family. She had a poor choice in men, that's all. Now this Curtis Thomas, he was a bullshit artist, as good as any he'd ever seen, and if a grand jury thought him good for the murder of his spouse, well, he would drive to hell and back to fetch a state's witness turned rabbit.

As a motivation, Burgoon had kept a letter the department chief had handed him one day last winter. Its author was anonymous, and it was delivered addressed only to the St. Louis Police Department and the Illinois State Police. It was dated February 3, 1995, four days after Curtis was arrested.

"*Thank you very much for pursuing the murder of Lynne Matchem-Thomas,*" it read in rounded cursive. "*I once knew Lynne and she was a beautiful African-American woman. Many times, we as black women believe that the larger community doesn't value our lives. But I know that there are many quality black women and men who work hard everyday. Although there are many injustices committed against us, I want you to know that I am grateful that you didn't just sweep her brutal murder*

213

under the rug..."

But he and Joe Nickerson weren't the only St. Louisans en route to Salem that day. Some St. Louis TV stations had gotten wind of the found woman and had already sent their reporters and camera crews. It must have been a slow news day.

"She was all upset and a little out of it," said Burgoon, recollecting the assignment about a year later. "She'd been in the field all night. The TV crews were outside, panting for an interview, so we took her out the back of the sheriff's office."

Still, her return made the evening news. The footage showed her embracing her distraught parents: "Deborah Claybrook is back home tonight. The missing woman was found safe near Salem, Illinois ..."

And this was the witness by whose testimony the case would turn.

FORTY-TWO

Pat Conroy was on Deborah Claybrook like a duck on a tick. During cross-examination, he assiduously tried to impeach her testimony, portraying her as a spurned lover, whose motive in testifying was to seek revenge against Curtis, whom, she had told a friend, "disregarded" her.

He played the journal up big. Actually, it was a date-book, a dark green Daytimer, which she used to keep track of appointments and such. This particular Daytimer, one for the year 1993, she had submitted to the police so they could lock in dates as pertained to her story. As evidence, it was the subject of much scrutiny, because it was notated with tantalizing comments about her romance with Curtis, and yet there was nothing in there about a murder or a confession of murder. Her explanation was that she could not set down anything incriminating, because he might read it and harm her.

With the actual datebook in her hand and photocopied pages of it in his hand, Conroy asked her to read the entries from specific dates. "Will you please read for the court what you wrote on May 5th, the day you went to Curtis' and saw Lynne there?"

Claybrook complied. "'Curtis married? Will I ever meet someone who doesn't lie or cheat?'"

"OK, now please go to May 18th and read what you wrote on that day."

She thumbed a few pages forward and read, "'Detectives about Curtis and Lynne. Legal advice? No more Curtis.'"

"Let's go to May 27th. What did you write on that day?"

Claybrook bristled. This was her personal book. It was not intended for the titillation of strangers. Nonetheless, she dutifully read: "'Spent day with Curtis. Walked on trail in Edwardsville. Good time! Curtis doesn't trust me. Found him looking through glove compartment of car. Why?'"

"Uh-huh," said Conroy from the defense table. He had positioned himself in such a way that she could not avoid looking at Curtis when she responded to the questions. "Now, on May 31st what did you write in your book?"

"'Spent day with Curtis. Nice!'"

"There is an exclamation point on the word 'nice.' Isn't that so?"

"I use a lot of exclamation points," she said.

"Now doesn't this entry coincide with Curtis'

216

alleged confession to you?"

"That's not what I said," she corrected.

"Then what did you say?"

"I said it was sometime at the end of May or the beginning of June."

"And how would you define that period?"

"From about May 15th to June 15th."

"Let's move along to June 11th. Please read that entry."

"'Break up? Curtis continues to be a womanizer and doesn't work well at covering his tracks. This is the last time I will see him again.'"

"I see," said Conroy coyly. "You are concerned about Curtis reading your datebook and seeing something about himself he doesn't like, and yet you write that he is a womanizer and you are ending the relationship."

Claybrook sat silent in the witness chair for about 15 seconds looking at Conroy. Finally, she said, "Is that a question?"

On June 17, Curtis' birthday, they had a late lunch at Two Black Cats, a West End cafe and bar. After, they went to Curtis' place and spent the remainder of the day there. When Curtis got a call from his brother's ex-wife, Pat, asking him out for a drink, he assented. At nine, Pat pulled up and honked the horn. Deborah assumed she was going along, until Curtis told her she was not invited. As the two drove off, Deborah Claybrook got in her car and drove home.

Conroy asked her to find the passage from that day. "Now what did you write?"

"I wrote, 'I am confused. Make one more attempt at working things out.'"

"This is June 17th, correct?"

"Yes."

"Curtis had already told you that he killed Lynne?"

Claybrook glanced at Curtis sitting there, shooting her the evil eye. She said he had.

"And yet," prompted Conroy, "you wanted to make one more attempt to work things out with a man who had cut his wife's head off ?"

"My reasoning for continuing to see Curtis was because, like I said, I felt it would be easier to befriend him so I would know what he was thinking and how he felt. I wanted him to end the relationship so he would not come around bothering me."

For the first time, Deborah Claybrook revealed her cunning. In her mind, Curtis was a murderer, calculating and dangerous, but she was playing him like a fiddle.

Conroy asked her to read her entry from July 3.

"'Parents went out of town. Curtis came to visit me this weekend. Nice!'"

"With an exclamation point, correct?"

"That's correct."

"So you had a nice weekend with a man who had just chopped his wife's head off ?"

She repeated her rationale that by staying close to him she was privy to his thoughts and moods. She was an espionage agent in the perilous field of wayward romance. Only the diligent gathering of intelligence would keep her from harm.

Though he had made his point, Conroy had her read selected entries all the way into late September. It painted a picture of a woman who seemed more concerned with being stung by a bad relationship than being physically harmed by a homicidal maniac. On

July 6, the occasion of being snubbed at the Eric Marenthal concert, she wrote, "Tonight have reached end of rope with Curtis. No turning back."

"Slipped back," she wrote on July 13. "When am I going to realize that Curtis only hurts me?"

"'Slipped back?'" barked Conroy. "Into the relationship? What does that mean?"

"I may have loaned him money, driven him to work, returned his calls, but I don't think it means we were back together."

Yet, a few weeks later she called him to help her move from her parent's home into an apartment. The entry for July 31 read, "Move things. Called Curtis. OK! Late, but helped."

On August 26, she wrote, "Heard from Curtis. Don't know!! Testing." Upon Conroy's insistence, she explained that Curtis had called and left a message, and she was at odds over what to do. She didn't know whether to put a moratorium on seeing him or see him occasionally, but not as a boyfriend.

And the reference to "testing"?

"I was being tested for AIDS," she explained. "I thought I may have contracted it from Curtis."

The datebook showed that over the next month the process of disattachment was completed.

August 31: "Talk to Curtis no more."

September 1: "End to relationship with Curtis."

September 7: "Spent day with Curtis. Not sure where it will go."

September 9: "Definite. Curtis will no longer be in my life."

September 21: "Heard from Curtis. Did not return call."

"Nearly four months of entries in your datebook relating to time spent with Curtis," said Conroy, rising from his chair. "And those entries clearly indicate that you left the relationship then came back to it. Left and came back again and again. Why would you do that? Why would you want to court this man whom you say was a killer, whom you were afraid of?"

Deborah Claybrook was not to be ruffled by this hostile attorney. She shrugged her shoulders and answered. "Some relationships," she said, "defy logic."

FORTY-THREE

Conroy did his best to totally flummox Claybrook. He bullied and badgered her. He made her cry. He would fire questions and not let her answer, until, finally, Judge Huber had to give him a rebuke: "You have been stopping her short and arguing with her. You may inquire into this area, but I am not sure she knows what you are talking about, and before she can answer, you go into some other question."

He seemed to think that repetitious, ambiguous questions would trip her up. For instance, she had already stated under direct exam that Curtis confessed to her one night in late May or early June, but Conroy, in his muddled quest for truth, had everyone scratching their heads.

"Now, you also said that — where in your grand jury testimony did you say that shortly after the police left, Lynne was murdered? Did you ever tell that to the grand jury?"

"That's not what I said," replied Claybrook. "Curtis told me that shortly after *I* left that first time on a Wednesday that he murdered her."

"All right," said Conroy. "So when are we talking about? When you left? Which time is it? Were you over at Curtis' house?"

Claybrook said yes to the last question.

"And this is the night that the police came?"

"I don't know. The police came many times."

"Let's put it this way: Do you recall the police coming that night?"

"What night?"

"The night that Curtis told you that after you left he murdered Lynne?"

"No, I don't recall the police coming."

Just as the cross-exam was starting to gain momentum, Conroy became obfuscatory. With a "humph" and a shuffle, he queried, "What, tell me this, what, you were at the house on Waterman?"

Claybrook said she was.

"You were with Curtis?"

Claybrook said she was.

"And were you aware that Lynne had disappeared?"

"At what point?"

"At this point we are talking about."

Dobrinic then broke in. "What point is it?" she wondered. "I'm confused."

Judge Huber asked him what point he was referring to. It turned out that Conroy was referring to the night of May 7, 1993, though he was the only one in the courtroom who knew it.

It was a grueling situation for Deborah Claybrook,

though she should not have expected anything less. Still, she must have been wholly disarmed when Conroy, out of the blue, asked her if she had "a substantiated alibi for when Lynne Thomas was killed."

This had the effect of tossing a cherry bomb at the prosecution.

"Objection!" cried Kathryn Dobrinic, bolting to her feet.

"Sustained!" echoed Judge Huber.

"Ask to have it be stricken and counsel admonished."

Pat Conroy shrugged resignedly, giving the court a look that said, "Well, you can't blame me for trying."

FORTY-FOUR

Juror No. 1317 had a persistent cough. It had started on the second day of trial, a mild clearing of the throat: "Unh, unnnh — unh, *unnnh*," followed by a dainty dab on the mouth with a blue Kleenex. But, as the days went on, it mutated into a wet, hacking fluegelhorn of a cough, the consumptive's hallelujah. In short, the court was recessed while the judge decided whether to replace her with an alternate or send the bailiff to the drugstore for a bottle of Robitussin. Let her chug some of that, eh? If it knocks her out at least she's quiet.

Some of the spectators stayed in, and some were outside lighting up. Smoking breaks were getting far and fewer between. The jurors, too, can smoke outside, but, of course, they have to keep to themselves, away from the non jurors and certainly out of earshot of any reckless comments which could taint the case.

The media was out in force, standing around, talking about the case like gossips at the backyard fence. Besides myself, there was Pete Baum from WSMI, a country radio station in Litchfield and Alma Snider from the *Hillsboro Journal*. It was amazing that this rural county would have two fishwraps — the *Journal* and the *Montgomery County News* — that publish regularly every other day by joint agreement. Equally amazing, considering the defendant was a St. Louisan, was the absence of a reporter from the *St. Louis Post-Dispatch*. The *Post* covered his arrest, but never the trial itself. The world would have to get the story from us second-stringers. We had just seen the riveting performance of Deborah Claybrook, and we were eager to discuss it.

"Would you buy a used car from that woman?" asked Snider

"That's the million-dollar question," said Baum, stroking a bearded cheek. "She acted sincere in court, but what if, for the sake of argument, she was lying on the stand, exacting revenge on Curtis for his womanizing, for his lying and cheating ..."

" ... and," I broke in, "for casually using her and then discarding her like a spent condom?"

"What if ?" said Snider.

"It was apparent from her testimony that she could be conniving," said Baum.

"I know Curtis somewhat," I offered, "and I can tell you straightaway that anyone who knows Curtis will have a hard time believing that he would admit to the crime, especially to a girlfriend. It's one thing to brag about ripping off a merchant, but quite another to tell an on-again, off-again fickle lover you committed a

225

murder, risk being turned in the first time you displease her."

"But he's so arrogant," said Snider, "that he might've just thought, 'I've got to tell someone, and she's in no position to hurt me.'"

"Why risk it?" I countered. "By telling her, she has power over him, not the other way around."

"He might have thought it would be more interesting if someone else knew," theorized Snider. "He seems like the kind of guy who'd toy with someone like that. What's a game without a challenge?"

"I don't know," said Baum, "very few people would play that kind of game — life in prison to the loser."

"So," said Snider, "back to the original question: What if ... ?"

"She would be guilty of the worst kind of perjury," I replied.

FORTY-FIVE

By the end of the trial Dobrinic had the haggard look of a boot camp recruit just off two weeks of KP. On the last day, just before luncheon recess, the pot boiled over and the vitriol spilled into the courtroom. It happened when Curtis took the stand. Dobrinic began questioning him about his criminal record, and Conroy adamantly objected.

At the sidebar, Conroy expressed dismay that the state would bring up Curtis' guilty plea to the Leather Bottle robbery. That was more than 10 years ago. But Dobrinic assured him the State did not intend to go back that far. There was another within the 10-year limitations; she would bring up that charge.

"What is it?" sputtered Conroy.

"Forgery conviction."

"This is new information."

"Your client's record is new information to you?"

It turned out the offense was insufficient funds.

Curtis had stopped payment on a check in 1987.

They argued for awhile. Conroy said that by bringing this up as a prior conviction she was violating the rules of discovery. Trial by ambush, he charged. She said she told him she was going to do it; he denied that.

The sidebar is a private conversation between judge and counsel. The remarks, recorded by the court reporter, are supposed to be hushed, but voices were being raised, and way in back you could make it out.

"He is an officer of the court," Dobrinic was saying. "He can tell the court I didn't tell him something, but we had a conversation in my office where he admitted his client has had one (prior) within the 10 years. We can use that, he said, but we couldn't use the armed robbery. He told that to me in my office."

"That's a lie!" spat Conroy, and he stamped off.

The trial transcripts do not show an exclamation point after that last declarative sentence, but it was there.

In the courtroom, Dobrinic rarely came across as intimidated, though for some reason when she knew she was getting beat on a certain issue or when emotions ran high her cheeks would flush a splotchy pink. If she were aware of this, say she happened to look in the mirror, it only made the condition worse. That day, Dobrinic returned after lunch, her face mottled, puffy, the color of a baboon's butt.

Criminal-defense attorneys say a defendant who can testify is a gift, but that's if the defendant presents himself as convincing and forthright. For example, you wouldn't want Richard Nixon to testify that the sun will rise tomorrow; people wouldn't believe him because, admit it, he looked shady. It was probably a mistake to let Curtis testify in his own behalf. Some people present made the observation that he did not "read well," for when he took the stand on the final day of trial he was not as sufficiently indignant as one might expect in a man falsely accused of murder. In some respects, a criminal trial is a game, albeit a serious game, complete with a set of rules, yes, but as for the winning of the game the effective use of histrionics may be as important as knowing the rules. And so, as a player in this game, Pat Conroy should have exhorted his client to be demonstrative.

"Get up on that witness stand," he might have said, "and act like you're totally outraged at the injustice that has been put on you. Show the jury with your body language and tone of voice that you're being rail-roaded. Convince them that you're as innocent as a baby in a basket."

But that was not Curtis' style. His style was to speak calmly, slowly and confidently, inadvertently giving off an air that might be construed as cavalier. His style was to appeal to the intellect rather than to the emotions.

Under direct examination by Conroy, he portrayed himself as a sensitive husband worried over his wife's unstable and deteriorating mental condition, though he did admit to feeling "guilty" about not helping Lynne until she had a "major breakdown," referring to her stay in Barnes' 15500. Curtis, whose phone was busy all that night as the ER staff tried to reach him, said in court that the episode caused a marked change in her personality.

"She wasn't the same Lynne I knew before," he remarked. "She was psychotic, delusional."

He speculated that Lynne's fate was the result of her mental illness; she had a history of going off for days at a time, her whereabouts a mystery. She could have gone anywhere after leaving his house. Most likely, she had followed some capricious urge and wound up in the wrong place at the wrong time.

In fact, there were two sets of gruesome murders in the St. Louis area that pertained to Curtis' case. One involved the decapitations of two black women in East St. Louis. The second decap occured in July 1992, and a suspect named Samuel Ivory was picked up a month later. He was tried, convicted and sentenced to life in prison (ultimately taking his own life in 1996). Decap murders are a rarity, an Old Testament-style of vengeance, but unfortunately for Curtis, Ivory was incarcerated at the time of Lynne's disappearance.

On the other hand, the Cherokee Street murders, a series of slayings involving white women, known prostitutes in some cases, whose bodies were found in trash bags and refuse containers on the side of the highway, was closer to the timeline in the Matchem-Thomas case. The perpetrator(s) of those homicides has never been caught.

Curtis responded to Conroy's questioning that Lynne told him she was seeing a man "and that it was love at first sight, that this was her soul mate and she was going to go off and live with him."

"How did that make you feel?" queried Conroy.

"I thought clinically," replied Curtis. "I thought that this is, this is an element of the mania. And so there was no argument, no attempt to dissuade her, but an attempt to monitor."

Monitor. An interesting choice of words. As if she, his estranged wife, were one of his clients at Holtwood.

"I think she needs a good-faith basis to make an objection. She can't object for the sake of objection." There was a bit of whine in his tone as Conroy appealed to Judge Huber. It was only a few minutes into Curtis' testimony, and Dobrinic had objected to Conroy's line of questioning a good half-dozen times.

Clearly, Huber's patience was wearing thin. He wagged his finger at Conroy and replied, "I think we've seen a lot of that during the trial from both sides. Now please continue with this witness."

Conroy sighed as if the weight of the world was on his shoulders. He was easily exasperated and quite demonstrative about it.

Regarding Claybrook, the jury heard a much different story from Curtis. They had dated casually in the mid-80s. Claybrook was, in fact, aware of his marriage and in 1988, when she learned of it, broke out the windows on his car. But if Curtis had any proof of this, it wasn't brought out at the trial.

"In the spring of 1993 our relationship recommenced," Curtis said, responding to Conroy's questioning. "It was not a serious romance," he remarked.

Why was that?

"I didn't want a steady girlfriend because there was a lot of baggage after dealing with Lynne, and I didn't want to go into a relationship with someone who was

... unstable," he said, kindly employing the euphemism.

Conroy had his forefinger to his temple. He massaged it gently, thoughtfully. He looked down at the floor and then back up at Curtis. "Did you ever feel that you have, for lack of a better phrase, bad taste in women?"

It was rich, this attempt to elicit sympathy for Curtis' "plight," as it were. The answer, however, was of no consequence, because the spectators in this trial had already come to the distinct conclusion that the central characters in this melodrama, city people with their unseemly ways, were a bunch of degenerate goofballs anyway.

FORTY-SIX

Dobrinic could barely conceal her contempt for the defendant — and that's what he was to her, not the sometimes social activist with a degree from Wash. U., not the hotshot player with scams to run and a string of concubines back home, but the *defendant*, a guy to be convicted.

Curtis took the stand for over three hours that Tuesday. In a calm, modulated voice, Curtis told Dobrinic that, yes, as a community-support worker he had taken the orange van during May 1993. It was part of his job, visiting clients assigned to him at different locations. On one occasion he signed out the van to help move a client during business hours. He said the keys, kept in a cupboard at Holtwood, were readily available. As for Mo Powell and Nancy Anderson seeing him drop off the van that Monday morning, they were mistaken. The passage of so much time had muddled their memories. It might have happened, he conceded, but not on that particular date, May 10, 1993.

He staunchly denied ever taking the van that particular Saturday night, ever setting foot in Litchfield, ever telling Deborah Claybrook that he killed Lynne and chopped off her head. He wasn't going to cop to any culpability whatsoever.

OK, but how to explain the news clips found in his home after he was taken into custody? They were dated from the first days of the investigation when the victim was thought to be Caucasian.

The news clips about the body were in his house because his mother had passed them along, he explained. The stories had reported that the victim was a nail-biter and had a fibroid tumor of the uterus. May Ruth knew Lynne had the same. It was so coincidental, these conditions, that she deeply suspected the dead girl was her daughter-in-law.

"And I explained to my mother," said Curtis from the stand, "that an anthropologist had determined that this woman was white, that she had borne children and that she was left-handed. Even so, my mother still thought it was Lynne. Black women have fibroid tumors, she said, white women don't."

May Ruth Thomas, however, could not attest to this. She had died of a heart attack in February while Curtis was in the St. Louis City Jail.

There were notations on the newspaper articles, jots and dates, that intrigued Dobrinic. Some were written in pencil, some in ink from a ballpoint. She wanted to show that he had been keeping close track of the case from the very start. These notations would prove that. She approached the witness, showed him the clippings taken from a drawer in his living room and now in evidence. How about this, she prodded, "'Decapitated Body Discovered Near Campground In Illinois.' Do you see any handwriting on that?"

"Yes."

"Whose is that?"

"Looks like my mother's."

She showed him another clipping. "Whose handwriting is that?"

"Looks like my mother's."

"Are you saying this handwriting was on these articles when you got possession of them?"

"The inkings are new to me. The dates, everything in pencil, I had seen. The things in ink I have never seen before."

"You're saying the things in ink weren't on this when the police took it out of your house?"

Curtis said he didn't know what was on there when the police took it out of his house — he was in custody, how could he know? He only knew that, when his mother gave him the clippings, all the handwriting was in pencil.

Dobrinic repeated the already-answered question. "Are you saying it was your mother's?"

"Yes, I am."

"And your mother is deceased?"

Dobrinic's tone was mocking, unmistakenly implying that Curtis would use his mother's death as an alibi.

"Well, I pick up on your sarcasm," said Curtis, icily. "My mother *is* dead. It's nothing to joke about."

"No sir," she agreed. "Death is nothing to joke about."

Au contraire. Black humor, sometimes called gallows humor, has a long tradition in literature. Voltaire was a

235

deft practitioner of the craft. Heller's *Catch-22* is steeped in comedic fatalism. Making light of death — not the cheap jokes about dead celebs, but when it's you, your life, at issue — is a coping mechanism for miserable or unbearable situations. Think of Oscar Wilde on his deathbed, having no choice but to gaze for days on end at the dreary wallpaper in his Parisian hotel room, and uttering with his last labored breath, "Wallpaper, one of us has got to go." A wry bon mot works at least as well as pathetic blubbering.

We are wired for humor, thank God. Humor lifts, redeems, distinguishes the human race. Death was nothing to joke about; death was everything to joke about. This trial and all the capricious events leading up to it was in fact a masterpiece of dark comedy.

FORTY-SEVEN

Curtis claimed his whereabouts were known and verifiable all day and night on Saturday, May 8, 1993. No one disputed that he was at work that day from 11 a.m. until 9 p.m. Or close to 9 p.m. It was the after-work hours that were nebulous. His alibi rested with two people: A co-worker, Gloria Ann Jones, to say he clocked out at 9 p.m., and a friend, Aaron Seymour, to say he picked up Curtis and took him straight home.

Curtis caught the bus to work on Saturday morning, arriving just before the late-morning shift change. Almost everybody was at the staff retreat so Curtis had the place much to himself. Jones, like Curtis, a resident assistant, checked in to Holtwood at 4 p.m., their shifts overlapping for five hours. On the witness stand, Jones said that she and Curtis worked in different parts of the facility, had different clients to attend to, and that while she would encounter him from time to time, there were long periods when she didn't see him at all. As for signing out, she said, there was no time clock at Holtwood. The system was based on honesty, the comings and goings entered on the schedule in the employ-

237

All I know is it wasn't cold out

ee's handwriting. No, she had not actually seen Curtis
sign out that evening, but departing employees usually
apprised their relief when they were getting ready to
leave, and, she said that Curtis normally complied with
that procedure.

Wasn't it possible, even easy, coaxed Conroy, for an
employee to leave work early? Jones admitted that
employees sometimes took advantage of the system, but
that these "early departures" were only a few minutes
prior to the authorized quitting time. She also denied
observing any pattern of early departures or late arrivals
on the part of Mr. Thomas.

Eleven to nine was not the normal shift at
Holtwood on a Saturday, but the retreat had caused a
change in scheduling, which, Curtis being without a
car, had put him out a little. In St. Louis County, the
buses are less regular on weekends, he explained to
Conroy from the witness stand. The Midland bus does-
n't run at all on Sundays, and on Saturdays it stops running around seven. He was scheduled to work at

Lohmeyer, another Independence Center facility, at eight the next morning, so he had to find a way home, get some sleep and then get up and do it again. He thought about taking a cab, but he didn't want to spend the money. He thought about borrowing one of the Center's vans — after all, it would be entirely work-related — but he didn't think that was proper. In the end, he arranged for his buddy, Aaron Seymour, to pick him up that night. Nine p.m. sharp.

But Seymour wasn't familiar with Overland, one of 90-some Balkan-like municipalities in St. Louis County, and he was late. Curtis was about to call a cab when Seymour finally pulled up. They went to a QuikTrip, bought some beer and went to Curtis' place.

"Did anyone see Mr. Seymour arrive to pick you up?" asked Conroy.

"Not that I know of."

"Then what happened?" pressed Conroy.

"Aaron's a nice guy and all," Curtis explained, "but he sometimes doesn't get the hint." He had to be to work in the morning, and the guy just wouldn't leave. They drank beer and joked around till late, very late. Curtis got up early that Sunday morning and, hung-over, caught the bus to Lohmeyer for the day shift.

That seemed reasonable.

But later that day Seymour would trip during cross-examination. Dobrinic put a full-court press on him, and his story just fell apart like a house of cards. He wasn't sure, after all, that he picked up Curtis on May 8, 1993. "It could have been June or July," Seymour said. "All I know is it wasn't cold out."

About this time, Curtis was seeing the cell doors clank shut.

FORTY-EIGHT

In his closing arguments, Conroy led off with a broad-side on the victim's foibles, starting with the alcohol in Lynne's system. "Now, if this had been some type of vehicular manslaughter prosecution," he intoned, "where the blood-alcohol content was what it was for Lynne Thomas, you think the State would run away from it as much as they have here? They don't have any reasonable explanation for how this woman was drunk and yet with this man. The State would have you believe that she was afraid of Curtis, didn't want to see him again, blamed him for her life being ruined. So why would she go out and get drunk with this man before he killed her? Ladies and gentlemen, the physical evidence cannot change, no matter how much they would like it to."

Rolling right along, Conroy launched into Lynne's promiscuity. "You had testimony from the State's own witness, the psychiatrist, that this woman had mental problems, that she had psychotic fits, that, most importantly, she had been sleeping with men other than Curtis, other than Martin Plummer — and we don't have any idea who this man is! The State never investigated it. And this is documented evidence from the State's witness, this isn't me coming up and saying the woman was sleeping around.

"And Martin Plummer, where is Martin Plummer? We have never seen him. We know he was intimately involved in a relationship with the victim, we know that he skipped town after she disappeared, and yet he has never been produced. Why? The State has the burden of proof. All they had to do was put him on the stand. They have no explanation for why he wasn't called as a witness."

But the most compelling arguments in Conroy's arsenal focused on three aspects: the timeline for the evening of May 8, 1993, the credibility of Deborah Claybrook and the decided lack of physical evidence.

"Now, the FBI went in to Curtis' house. They spent two days and thousands of dollars in their exhaustive search, and you know very well that if they would have found any evidence, the smallest drop of blood, you would have heard about it. That FBI report alone is enough to exonerate this man."

With that, he made a nice segue. "The State is in the strange position of arguing that somehow Curtis is smart enough to have conceived this plan where he doesn't leave a trace of blood in the van, doesn't leave a trace of blood in the house, yet at the same time he evidently runs his mouth to everybody. Now, which one is it? Is he the cold, calculated, psychopathic killer, or is he the person that continued to show concern over his wife's disappearance?"

Then he turned to the problem of Deborah Claybrook. For all her schemes and intrigues she would make Machiavelli look like a boy scout. First off, she concocted Curtis' so-called confession.

"There isn't one detail in her story," Conroy said to the attentive jurors, "that she couldn't have got out of the paper. Correction, there is one detail that was not in the paper — about the gasoline. She said the body was doused in gasoline, and she got that wrong! Now, she presumed there was gasoline because the body was ablaze, and that's why she said it. She had no way of knowing that the State did forensic analysis of it and showed that there *weren't* any accelerants. Oh, I'm sorry, the officer testified that there *may* have been accelerants. They could put a thousand policemen on the stand and say, 'Well, there are no accelerants, but they could be there.' You know, if they had found the slightest trace of any gasoline on that woman you would have heard about it."

Secondly, the St. Louis Circuit Attorney's office spurned her initially and with good reason.

"The State's Attorney here is trying to make the city prosecutor's office down in St. Louis look like the Keystone Cops, that they would casually dismiss the story of a woman who comes along and says, 'Oh yeah, I am a material witness to a homicide, and I am afraid for my life.' Do you really think it reasonable that if they had the slightest belief in her story that they would not have pursued it or offered her protection? What does that say about her testimony?

"And what does it say about a woman who drove a car into a soybean field and lived there for two or three days because unknown people were following her? The state police checked it out and they found nothing, *nothing* mind you, because nobody was chasing this woman. You heard what she had to say. This is a woman who had, by her own admission, mental problems."

He was warming up now. "Now the motive for Deborah Claybrook is very simple. It is actually to be found in her book of private thoughts, her datebook: 'Will I love somebody who doesn't lie or cheat?' It's the oldest story known to man. You cross your lover, and she tries to get back at you. Shakespeare wrote about it 400 years ago: 'Hell hath no fury like a woman scorned.'

"And this story about how she was afraid of Curtis and how she had to pretend affection so as not to tip him off that she was going to the police. Well, here's something to consider." Conroy held up a legal pad and squinted at it. "'Curtis continues to be a womanizer who doesn't work well at covering his tracks. This is the last time I will ever see him again,'" he read dramatically.

"That's in her handwriting dated June the 11th. Is that consistent with the testimony she gave you? If she really were afraid of him, why would she write something like that knowing he might see it? Then on July 5th, 'No more intense time with Curtis.' July 13th: 'When am I going to learn that Curtis only hurts me?' These are not flattering comments. Now, they may be *truthful* comments, but that doesn't make him a murderer because she comes along and says it's so."

If she was piqued enough to openly gripe about Curtis in her private datebook, then why was there no mention of the horrible things he had told her? It was a good point, and Conroy drove it home for the second time. The attorney went back to squinting at his legal pad. "June 17th, Curtis' birthday. She has a little sticker, 'birthday.' She is going to celebrate the birthday of a man who already supposedly confessed this absolutely hideous murder. June 20th: 'Pick up Curtis from work.' July 3rd: 'Curtis comes to visit, nice!' Is that reasonable? Again, she explains it by saying that if she wrote anything that he might see and think incriminating that he might do her harm. She would trick him into believing she cared for him. And despite this fabrication, the State has no choice but to embrace her story and stand up for her.

"And Curtis, he is like a character in an old Jerry Lewis movie. It's called *The Patsy*, because that's what he is. Admittedly, he has poor judgment with women, but that doesn't make him a killer."

Conroy was certainly working up a lather. Perhaps more than any other time during the trial, he had the jury in his grasp. Closing remarks may have been his forte. Now he would hammer away at the time line. This was a case where minutes mattered. Could Curtis have had time to drive the body to Lake Lou and be there as early as 10:15? Conroy would say that it was a tight fit, a very tight fit, unless he sped there, and why do that? You speed on the interstate, you may get pulled over. If the prosecution's scenario was correct, he'd had her body concealed for three days, so why rush to get rid of it?

"Now do you have any testimony that the records were not accurate with what time Curtis worked? Ann Jones came here, and she told you that Curtis was there when she got to work and he checked out at 9 o'clock that night. That's uncontroverted testimony. Now, everybody agrees that Curtis didn't have a car. So how would he get off his shift at nine, somehow get to his house on Waterman, load a body into a van on a Saturday night, a half-block from a main thoroughfare in St. Louis, and then drive the 60 miles to Litchfield all within the time that the State has laid out? He is a very fortunate man in that he was working and has a record of his time.

"Physical evidence," spoke Conroy, "that's what I want you to look at. Where is the head? Where is the murder weapon? The bloody clothes? If you believe the State's theory, Curtis has got the body in the basement while he is entertaining a guest upstairs, someone who has free reign of the house. What was to keep her from walking down into the basement while the police were there? Is it really believable that this man would create this elaborate scheme where he eliminates his wife and then starts inviting people over while the body is rotting in the basement?

"And you heard the testimony from the psychiatrist, that Lynne Thomas was not psychotic before she was in his care. He does what doctors do all the time now, they give you drugs: 'Here, have some pills.' And he said, you know, there was a 'finite possibility' that she could have a manic episode from those drugs. It turned out that way, didn't it? He admitted that the drugs caused her to have psychotic episodes. Did you see any sign of regret? No. You see him trying to pawn off his incompetence on the defendant."

If he was going to win this case, he was going to have to skewer the victim a bit. "And isn't it strange that a woman who has never had serious psychological problems, as soon as she is released from the psych ward of a hospital, after she is given these powerful drugs, starts having bouts, for the first time in her life, of 'hypersexuality.' This is from the psychiatrist who testified that she was sleeping around — not just with Curtis or Martin Plummer but with unknown other people whom the State has failed to produce. And this is not me calling the woman a slut. Lynne Thomas had severe psychological problems due to her medication — the doctor admitted it, and after she reports to him that she is sleeping with other men, 'impulsively,' I think was his word, she disappears and turns up dead. You know she was in East St. Louis. You know she got in a fight in some nightclub there. You got that from the doctor. There was evidence of alcoholic blackouts. And yet all these problems are supposed to point to him?"

He played on the jurors' presumed mistrust of big-city ways. "You heard Detective Sheeley testify to unsolved crimes in this country, similar unsolved crimes where women are decapitated. That's a terrible thing today; women are vulnerable people. They can be easy victims, especially in a city like St. Louis. And you have all been to St. Louis at some point. It's not like here. It's a metropolis of two-and-a-half million. If you are going to East St. Louis nightclubs, if you are out sleeping with men you just met, if you are having trouble with drugs ..."

"I object to things that aren't in evidence," Dobrinic interjected. She hadn't been objecting terribly much during Conroy's speech.

"These *are* in evidence," Conroy retorted. The judge did not agree.

Conroy sighed and continued. "If you are going to be the type of person that puts yourself in those situations, these things happen. This crime will never be solved. The killer is out there."

There was more. The fact that Curtis had no known ties to the Litchfield area. The fact that there was a discrepancy between the witnesses' description of the suspect van and the Independence Center van that Curtis was supposed to have driven. The fact that he knew Lynne had been a security guard; they had even gone downtown together when she was fingerprinted. If he was bent on going to so much trouble to keep the body from being identified, why did he not cut off the hands, too?

Patrick Conroy wound up his impassioned peroration with a plea to set Curtis free.

"Now, this man has lost his wife, he has lost his freedom. Give him back his freedom. Give him back his life."

FORTY-NINE

In closing arguments, the State goes first, then the defense and, lastly, the State's rebuttal. The State gets the final word because it has the burden of proving beyond a reasonable doubt every element of the crime of concealing a homicide. To do this, Kathryn Dobrinic was going to have to come out swinging like a prizefighter.

The prosecutor had a bounty of iniquities from which to draw her closing remarks, a sort of calendar of incriminating actions. To wit: April 27, 1993, defendant assaults spouse at hospital.

"Now, the defendant testified that his wife was suffering from a mental illness. She was going through a hard time, and he was very caring about her situation. And this is a person who is supposedly a professional, who works helping the mentally ill. But what happened in front of St. Mary's Hospital? He attacks her. He wrestles the keys of the car away from her, bites her on the shoulder and pushes her out of the moving car. He says in his statement he was 'disgruntled' because his wife had rented a car. She wasn't even living with him anymore, he is going to divorce her, ladies and gentlemen, so what's it to him whether she rents a car? He spent a long time in his testimony talking about how concerned he was over all her mental problems, but his actions belie that concern."

The incident, Dobrinic told the jury, was part of an established pattern of aggression that Curtis' displayed toward his wife. It went toward motive "to do those things in Litchfield."

Move on up to May 5 of that year. Victim last seen arguing with defendant in front of his home, a fairly incriminating scenario on the surface, especially in light of the third party present.

Dobrinic picked up on her remarks: "Now, ladies and gentlemen, you can believe if you want to that the only reason Deborah Claybrook was over at the defendant's house was to talk about his resume. Believe that if you care to, but I submit to you that the defendant was upset with Lynne for showing up when he had a date coming. And in fact, he wouldn't let Lynne in the house; he testified to that. She knocked on the door, and he wouldn't let her in. Yet, she is there when this woman comes over and she is still there when this woman leaves. Once again, she has messed things up for him. Lynne, the person who is causing him all these problems with her mental condition. Lynne, the person whose health insurance he is saddled with paying for. Lynne, the person he has worked up these divorce papers on. But he's around her this May 5th."

Step ahead one more day. Defendant calls in missing

report on wife.

"You heard from Judith Whitner, who works for the St. Louis Police Department and she testified that she called back the person leaving a message at 11:54 a.m. on May 6, 1993. She said that she talked to a person identifying himself as Curtis Thomas, that he told her Lynne was missing and that he gave Ms. Whitner certain information as to Lynne's description and what she was wearing.

"Well, ladies and gentlemen, this woman hadn't been living with him, he was getting divorce papers on her. In fact, in his testimony he said she would leave for days, her whereabouts unknown to him, so why is he calling the police to report her missing? I think the reasonable conclusion is, ladies and gentlemen, to put the suspicion off him, because he knew she wasn't missing, because he knew she wasn't ever going anywhere."

Continuing her chronology, the prosector came to May 7. Defendant stops police from searching his basement. Well, he was within his rights to do so, but doesn't it make you wonder?

She then went to the most compelling piece of circumstantial evidence yet. "The defendant worked at a place with a van matching a description of a van seen at the lake the night the body was found. What a coincidence," she added, with a dash of sarcasm.

" ... The kids all saw the van. They remembered it a little differently, but they still give pretty accurate descriptions considering the vehicle we find later in this story. They all looked at the photos and said, yes, this looks like the van we saw, maybe not in every detail, but they agreed on the type and make. They're talking about a Ford van, cargolike, heavy-duty wheels, reddish-orangish with Missouri plates — the very same type of van the defendant could have taken and, in fact, did take from his place of employment.

"And let's take a look at the time window for the events that evening. John Reeves said he saw a Ford van at Picnic Area No. 5 at 10:23. A fire hadn't started yet. Minutes later, the kids came around, and, at varying intervals, they saw this fire and the van. Now, the records show the defendant reported to work in the morning and that his shift went until 9 o' clock at night. However, Gloria Jones, the only other employee at Holtwood on that date, testified that she has no recollection of seeing the defendant at the time he left.

"The defendant comes and says, 'Oh yeah, I worked until nine, and then I went out beer-drinking with my buddy, who was late in picking me up.' But what's the reasonable conclusion? The reasonable conclusion, ladies and gentlemen, is that he got the van he needed. Because he didn't have a car, and so he's got to find some way to transport that body. And what he did — the reasonable inference from all the evidence in this case is — that he got that van, he put the body in the van, whether it was during work, after work, whenever, and he drove to Litchfield Lake and then dumped that body in a box with some plastic bags and he set fire to it.

"The question remains, did he have the time to do this? Well, please recall that Detective Sheeley told you that he started from the defendant's home and drove to the lake site where the body was found. And we are not saying that we know the exact route traveled, but the route Mr. Sheeley took, up Interstate 55, is the most direct route, so it is a reasonable experiment to try.

251

And the result is that it takes an hour and 10 minutes if you obey the speed laws. This fits well into that window of time that I talked about, where John Reeves said where he was at 10:23 and where the kids say they were at about 10:30. All these pieces dovetail, ladies and gentlemen. He had the opportunity to get rid of that body here, and he certainly had a lot of motive to get rid of that body here and not in the city of St. Louis."

If the State of Illinois v. Curtis L. Thomas did not have a smoking gun at least it had a warm derringer.

The rest was more or less cake decoration. May 10, 1993: Co-workers see defendant return missing van, never checked it out or in. May 14: Defendant collects news articles about the headless body. May 21 (or before): Defendant cancels victim's medical insurance policy, uses missing report to do so. Late-May/early-June 1993: Defendant confesses crime to Deborah Claybrook. May 1994 (or before): Defendant tells LuAnne McPherson that police have taken him to Litchfield to identify a headless body there. August 1994: U-Haul boxes that originated at defendant's house match design and thickness of moving boxes found at crime scene. August 1994: Defendant lies to Detective Sheeley regarding knowledge of van and of woman friend, "Claypool."

Certainly, it was a lot to pile on one person. Curtis, sitting there, listening to this litany of villanies attributed to him, did not make faces or otherwise indicate frustration with overt body language. Rather, a pensive state seemed to come over him, a look of world-weariness perhaps, possibly resignation.

Finally, Kathryn Dobrinic stopped pacing, caught

her breath and realized she was through. She looked at the jury hard and long; she pivoted in the direction of the bench and doing a sort of curtsy, said, "State rests, your honor."

Late in the afternoon, the jury got their instructions and went off to deliberate. The responsibility of Pat Conroy was at an end. It was time for 12 men and women to go into seclusion to try to answer the question of what Curtis Thomas was doing at or about 10:23 p.m. on May 8, 1993.

FIFTY

We were waiting for the verdict in Hillsboro's Church Street Pub, an old-time Methodist church restored to the blasphemous incarnation of an ale house. Waxing toward inebriation, our party of three speculated on the proceedings in the airy manner of armchair jurists.

"Maybe he did it and doesn't remember it," I offered. "Well, that's a friend's theory. She says that the mind can get so psychotic when truly incensed that it blanks out and doesn't remember committing murder. She's some kind of shrink, so it must be true."

"Oh, he knows what he did," said Pete Bastian. "He's too calculating not to know. What bothers me is that they haven't proven the homicide. The homicide is an element of the crime. The Supreme Court says if the State doesn't prove every fact constituting every element of the crime beyond a reasonable doubt, the defendant walks. If he's convicted, the conviction may be turned over on appeal."

I said that the dearth of blacks in Central Illinois could bolster Curtis' plea of innocence. "The question has to've crossed every juror's mind: Why would he risk dumping a body in a place where, if noticed, he'd stand out like a raisin in a bowl of sugar?"

"Because he's a sick and twisted individual?"

"Because he's got the balls of a bull moose?"

We laughed and ate for a while. "But you know," I resumed, "the other thing that really bothers me is John Reeves' testimony. That guy is a stickler for accuracy. He was so specific in his statement made the day after the body was discovered. If he said the van had no windows I tend to believe him."

Leible made a face that said I was a dufus. He said, "Yet how very weird that a van so similar but distinctly different from the one Curtis occasionally drove would be at the lake that night, an hour from St. Louis, dumping the body of Curtis' wife."

That was another thing. The time frame was a shoehorn fit, probably even tighter than Conroy had stressed. In actuality, whether Curtis could have gotten to Lake Lou within the established time limits really depended, in theory, on where Curtis had kept the body while working that Saturday. Was it in the van or concealed somewhere on the grounds so he could leave right after work? Or did he go home to get it?

"By the way," I offered. "I did the drive from Holtwood to Curtis' house. It was 7.4 miles through mostly commercial territory. On a weekday afternoon, it took 14 minutes, a time which included being stopped at three of the 12 traffic signals along the way. Say our guy got lucky with the stoplights and subtract two minutes: This 12-minute side trip puts Curtis farther away from I-70, the most direct route from Olivette to Litchfield. Say he left work at 9 p.m. in the van. This little trip home would be pushing the drive time to impractical limits — 65, maybe 55 minutes from St. Louis' West End to Lake Lou. Plus, he would have used the Poplar Street Bridge with its never-ending construction and backups."

"There was that parked car he drove away from Midland House that Monday morning as Anderson and Powell watched," reminded Bastian. "He's smart enough, he may have put the corpse in the trunk of that car, parked it nearby *before* he went in to work, and then when he gets off that evening he only has to park the van next to the car and transfer an ordinary-looking plastic trash bag. Quick and simple."

"Well he's not *that* damn smart," I replied. "People give him too much credit. I mean if Curtis was so smart, he would have known that he didn't need to call a lawyer to stop the cops from searching his house. He could have done that himself at any time. And if he did do the crime, it wasn't very smart to report Lynne as missing so soon when she wasn't even living with him."

"Nor was it smart to pack the body in boxes which could be traced back to him," chimed in Leible. "Nor was it smart to cancel her insurance only days after she's disappeared or to be seen by his co-workers driving a van he wasn't supposed to have, a van the police were looking for."

"Actually," said Bastian, "Curtis had a good reason to cut off her insurance while she was alive, to cut her off from the pill-pushers."

"Wow," said Ron Leible, hoisting a half-filled stein, "we're really cutting through the fog here. The whole thing is coming into focus."

"Yeah, well here's a monkey wrench for you," I said. "Another thing that really nags is the feeling in my gut that the method of handling the corpse, the mutilation and disfigurement, was a white-guy thing to do. What do you think?"

"Kind of like trailer trash, if you'll pardon the expression?" said Leible.

"At least someone who's not unaccustomed to hunting or fishing," I replied, "who can skin a deer or filet a bass and not think anything of it. Someone who would have the cold-bloodedness and presence of mind to chop or saw off a woman's head."

"You know, it's true," said Leible, "or at least it seems true, that most serial killers and doers of the really grisly murders are white guys."

"Manson, Bundy, Son of Sam ..." I offered.

"The Reverend Jim Jones and his electric Kool-Aid," said Leible. "The guy racked up over 900."

"You want into get into clergy?" from Bastian. "We'll go back to the counterfeit popes and all the bloodshed that caused."

"OK," I said, "how about the guy who whacked all those customers in the San Ysidro McDonald's about 10 years ago?"

"White guy lashing out," said Bastian.

"McVeigh?"

"He's not convicted."

"He's as good as fried."

"Get the picture?

In the end it was not unlike the O.J. trial. Either

you believed the defendant or you accepted the circumstantial evidence mounted against him. Would Curtis' dispassionate testimony dent the impression that the State's witnesses made? Toward which precipice would the jury make their leap of faith?

After four hours' deliberation, the jury filed back into the courtroom. Curtis entered through the same door a minute later, sandwiched between Conroy and Sheriff Vazzi. You had to hand it to Curtis. He always kept a bounce in his step, even now. Judge Huber asked Curtis to rise while the judge went through the rigamarole of reading the charges, two counts of concealment of a homicidal death — the hiding and the burning. The count of concealment by decapitation had been dismissed that very morning for the same reason the murder charges were dropped: out of jurisdiction. Curtis arose, smoothing the sides of his sport coat. Outwardly, he was the definition of cool; inwardly, well, that was between him and the Maker in whom he did not believe.

Then the judge directed the jury foreman, a jug-eared fellow with deep-set eyes and sagging jowls, to stand and deliver the verdict.

"How find you, the jury?" he intoned. The question hung in the air for a very long two seconds before the foreman answered back, "Your honor, we find the defendant Curtis Thomas guilty on both counts of concealment of a homicide."

He took it like a man. He held his head up and didn't flinch or wince or scream obscenities. He stood there defiant, haughty, glaring first at the judge, then the prosecutor, and then jury. Most of them looked away. Conroy put a paternal and consoling hand on his shoulder.

By macabre coincidence, the verdict was returned on Halloween night.

Nine hundred two days had passed from the discovery of the burned and mutilated body to the conviction of her husband.

As Shakespeare said, the wheels of justice creak slowly, and for all involved — the victim's family and friends, the prosecutors and detectives in two states, as well as the defendant and his champions — this justice carriage with its worn axle and rusted wheels had taken a long and circuitous route. Yet, to its destination it arrived as surely as the gavel sounds "court adjourned."

FIFTY-ONE

On the day of his sentencing, Curtis entered the courtroom, the trace of a smile on his mug. He stood before Judge Huber and pronounced the entire trial a sham.

"It seems like I was being convicted the day I arrived," he spoke. "The agreement seems to be 'since we can't get Mr. Thomas for murder, we'll get him for something and give him as much time as possible ...'

"Now that might be great for Central Illinois politics. I realize the filing started today for spring elections and all this makes great press ..."

Kathryn Dobrinic rolled her eyes. Certainly it galled her, the defense's repeated insinuations that Curtis was being made to play the patsy for her political ambitions. The primary election was four months away and she was up for retention. The sensational nature of the crime, the timing of the trial, the media coverage — the sentencing made the front page of the *Chicago*

Tribune — all of it calculated to fuel her naked push for power. It was a politician's world, Curtis maintained, and he was a pawn in their game.

"... but I resent being used as a chess piece, especially since that piece is the odious black chess piece."

It was a fine speech. Curtis railed against the system that convicted him. To support this contention, he could point to several things: the fact that most of Conroy's motions, including change of venue, were denied and that the all-white jury, ranging in years from middle-aged to elderly, was comprised of anything but his peers.

"I thought I was coming to Montgomery County, Illinois," said Curtis, waxing mighty indignant, "instead I found Montgomery, Alabama, circa 1955."

Ardently, Dobrinic rebutted Curtis' allegations. He wasn't being used, he was being convicted for doing something horrible. If anyone showed a racist attitude, it was he, Curtis Thomas. He chose Montgomery County as the hiding place for his wife's body, thinking perhaps that the murder of a black woman would not interest the authorities in a mostly white and rural county. Instead, Dobrinic noted, the case was pursued to the fullest, and Lynne Matchem-Thomas was buried with full Christian services, the coffin *and* burial plot donated by the people of Montgomery County.

Shirley Matchem was present. She had prepared a victim's statement to be read in court this day. The judge told her, go ahead, read it aloud. Shirley cleared her throat, and began haltingly, "My name is Shirley Matchem. I am the mother of the deceased, Lynne D. Matchem-Thomas. Because of the defendant, Curtis Thomas, I have no daughter. Curtis Thomas violated

I resent being used as a chesspiece

my daughter's right to live. Curtis Thomas was cruel, insensitive, uncaring, revengeful and cold. In other words, he had a shadowy appearance. He caused my family grief, put more depression on us. He doesn't seem to have any remorse for the offense he did to my daughter.

"Curtis Thomas should get the maximum sentence for the two counts on which he has been convicted. I thank the prosecuting attorney, Kathryn Dobrinic, the agent, Michael Sheeley, Detective Rich Burwitz, and the judge, Dennis M. Huber, who worked diligently to solve the case. I thank the jury for bringing in the guilty verdict."

She sat down. It was time for the sentence to be pronounced, and Curtis arose. He stood there in the harsh light of public condemnation, sharing a commonality with every other felon who had stood warily before the bench since Dismas, the good thief, was condemned to death by Pilate. At one time Curtis had thought he could get only five years, but he was misled. The state had upped the ante.

"This being an exceptionally brutal and heinous concealment," Dobrinic had asked the judge before trial to invoke the extended term provision if Curtis were convicted. An "extended term" is prosecutor talk for double time. On December 11, 1995, he was sentenced to 10 years in prison, double the normal maximum.

Kathryn Dobrinic had her verdict, but the sound of it rang hollow. She wanted the jackpot, not the consolation prize. "We did everything we could under the law," she told the gathered press, "and though the facts of this case won't permit us to prosecute for murder, we feel strongly that somebody should."

And somebody would.

FIFTY-TWO

The historic homes along the 5700 block of Waterman Avenue in St. Louis' fashionable West End share the same architectural plan — three-story, red-brick, single-family dwellings; front yard, back yard, porch. The home where Curtis lived with his wife for six years is no different from the rest, except for the dark secrets it may hold.

The home is presently occupied. Some nights you drive by, and the colorful custom-made address plate is lighted. Below the four-digit address you note the chemical symbol H_2O adjoins the universal symbol for man, a circle with an arrow pointing diagonally outward. Water + man = Waterman Avenue. It's clever, whimsical. It's the same rebus Curtis drew for Lynne in the library where they first met. The one that caught her eye.

───·•◆•·───

Six miles north of Litchfield up Old Route 66 there's a place called Honey Bend. It's not on the map; blink your eyes and you'll miss it. There's an RV Park, a topless club open nightly in a red barn, and a cemetery. That's about it. The cemetery is called Cedar Ridge. It is a small cemetery, an old and beautiful place, nestled in the shade of mature pine trees. I went to the white frame house on the southern edge of the property and knocked at the door. Anna Ragland answered. I told her what I wanted.

"Lester," she called, "somebody here looking for a grave."

Lester Ragland walked me to the graveyard proper. Lester's in his 70s, been living on this land as caretaker for more than 40 years. He is a talker, and he'll talk as long as you want to listen. He'll tell you the Ragland family plot has 19 interments, including his own son David, a Marine corporal, who returned from VietNam and just didn't feel right for the next 25 years. David died in 1994 from complications of Agent Orange — so they believe.

"It's a shame about that girl," said Lester, standing off to the side of Lynne's grave. "I'm glad they got the one that done it — her husband, wasn't it? I remember the police, that Agent Sheeley, brought the mother and some other women here to see it — the first time seeing it, you know — and the mother laid on the grave, just laid there, and she didn't cry. She screamed."

Lynne's grave has two headstones in Cedar Ridge Cemetery, probably the only one that does. The later headstone, put in after she was identified, bears her full name, the dual dates that punctuated her life, and the word "Daughter." But the first headstone, placed when she was still known only as Janie Doe, has a fitting epitaph, conceived by the wife of one of the state troopers on the case.

It reads, "In The Violent World Around Us, In God She Is Secure."

POSTSCRIPT

The following statement is contained in the four-volume case file of Curtis Thomas. The account is handwritten on an office memorandum of the Illinois State Police. It is reproduced verbatim, and the italics are those of Trooper Leach.

To: Inspector R.E. Burwitz
From: Tpr Charles J. Leach #4346
Date: 06/06/95
Subject: 05/08/93 Janie Doe Case - Associated Van

Sir,
This memo is intended to provide a written statement of my recollections regarding a suspect red/orange Ford van in connection with the Janie Doe Case. You have a copy of my field report #F-18-93-324. This information is not included:

On 05/08/93 at about 10:45 p.m. I was on duty, in my marked I.S.P. squad car. I was in my car parked at the curb in front of my home at 721 N. Jackson St., Litchfield (3 blocks north of IL 16). I was talking with my wife, across the sidewalk in my yard, through my open window.

At about 11:00 p.m. I started south on N. Jackson St. toward IL 16, intending to resume I-55 patrol. At IL 16 / N. Jackson intersection I had to wait for passing W/B traffic prior to turning right (W/B toward IL 16). I recall observing a W/B Ford van. My specific observations: red/orange in color, heavy duty suspension, no external markings, Missouri truck registration plates, steel mesh cargo protection screen behind driver, paint faded. I specifically recalled the van because I considered it "out of place" and looked it over for equipment violations (none noted).

I turned right onto W/B IL 16 and was the 2nd car behind the van. We stopped for a red signal at the State St. intersection and I looked at the back of the van, noting the heavy duty offset rear wheel/tire (left side). We continued W/B IL 16 through Litchfield. I noted no illegal driving patterns and decided to "dismiss" the van from further observation. Traffic was heavy.

I *think* the van turned right at the IGA/Hardee's intersection. I also *think* that I saw 2 male occupants.

I continued to I-55 and started S/B. After about 2 miles, at time 11:04 p.m., I was dispatched to Lake Lou Yeager to secure the Janie Doe scene.

EPILOGUE

Shirley Rogers made good on her promise to retry the defendant on the original charges. Curtis Thomas did just six months in the Illinois State Penitentiary before being reindicted for first-degree murder by a St. Louis grand jury. Consigned as a prisoner to the city jail in May 1996, he went to trial in the Municipal Courts, Division 22, on January 30, 1997, precisely two years after the day he was arrested for the murder of his wife. The first day of the trial there was a bomb threat, and everyone had to leave the building to stand outside in the cold for an hour while a bomb-sniffing dog did its duty.

Public defenders Sharon Turlington and Will Goldstein argued the case before Circuit Judge Booker T. Shaw. Assistant Circuit Kellee Concki called many of the same witnesses as were called by Kathryn Dobrinic during the Hillsboro trial. In fact, the Montgomery County State's Attorney, re-elected a few months after Curtis' conviction, had come down for the trial. She was in attendance every day, always in the front pew on the prosecution's side. Pat Conroy dropped in as well. He would stay for a few minutes, watching the proceedings and then leaving as quickly as he came. Once he walked in while Goldstein was grilling Deborah Claybrook about her datebook; it must have been sheer deja vu.

The jury, comprised of four blacks and eight whites, mostly in their 50s and 60s, weighed the same basic testimony from the same parade of witnesses. The same exhibits were trucked out as State's evidence. This time, however, Curtis did not take the stand in his own behalf. If he had, the prosecution could have impeached him with his own conviction, and his goose certainly would have been cooked. Likewise, though case notes permitted, the State declined to introduce the previous conviction. Prosecution wanted to play it safe and avoid a possible reversal of verdict.

Curtis appeared to be almost cheerful throughout the four-and-a-half day trial. At least his family members showed up this time around. With a racially-mixed jury and a pretty defender to put her hand on his shoulder periodically, as if to say, "See? This man is not an animal," I believe Curtis really thought he would be acquitted. The jury got the case around noon on a Wednesday, and three hours later they returned with a guilty verdict.

Judge Shaw, just before sentencing, produced a letter from Shirley Matchem. "The victim's mother would like information on the whereabouts of her daughter's head," spoke the judge. "For her peace of mind, she asks that you divulge what you did with it."

"That's assuming that I have it," Curtis blustered. "She should ask the murderer."

Under the charges of first-degree murder the only sentence available was life in prison without the possibility of parole. Curtis Lee Thomas is doing hard life in the Crossroads Correctional Center, Cameron, Missouri, over near St. Joseph. It is pretty country around there — farmland and gently rolling hills. Perhaps the quietude of rural environs has a settling effect on the prisoners. Hard life is an eternity; inmate No. 526964 digging in for the long, slow fade.

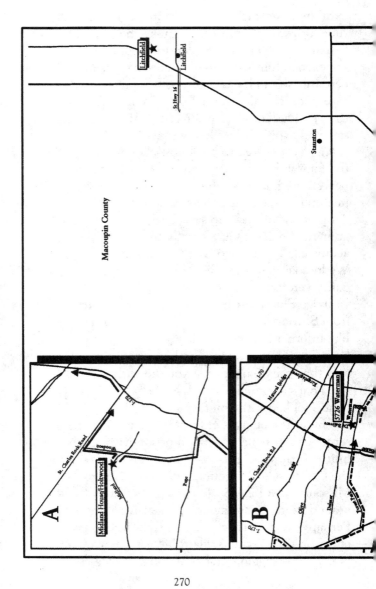

Macoupin County

Litchfield

Litchfield

St Hwy 16

Staunton

A

Midland House/Holwood

St. Charles Rock Road

Woodson

Midland

Page

I-270

B

I-270

5726 Waterman

Natural Bridge

Kingshighway

Waterman

Bellevue

St. Charles Rock Rd

Page

Olive

Delmar

I-170

270